The
LOST
BALLERINA

Deanna Lynn Sletten

The Lost Ballerina
A Novel

Copyright 2025 © Deanna Lynn Sletten

ISBN–13: 978-1-941212-96-7

Cover Designer: Deborah Bradseth

Novels by

Deanna Lynn Stetten

HISTORICAL

The Last Lady of the Silver Screen
Mrs. Winchester's Biographer
The Secrets We Carry
The Ones We Leave Behind
The Women of Great Heron Lake
Miss Etta
Night Music
Finding Libbie

WOMEN'S FICTION

The Heart of the Matter
The Lifestyle
Christmas at Mountain View Lodge
The Christmas Charm
One Wrong Turn
Maggie's Turn
Summer of the Loon
Memories
Sara's Promise

MURDER/MYSTERY

Rachel Emery Series
The Truth About Rachel
Death Becomes You
All the Pretty Girls

ROMANCE

Destination Wedding

Lake Harriet Series
Under the Apple Blossoms
Chasing Bailey
As the Snow Fell
Walking Sam

Kiss a Cowboy Series
Kiss a Cowboy
A Kiss for Colt
Kissing Carly

YOUNG ADULT

Outlaw Heroes

The
LOST
BALLERINA

CHAPTER ONE

Madison

Madison Carlson stood at the end of the long driveway, staring at the home that all the teens in the neighborhood believed was haunted. Oak and birch trees crowded the edges of the cracked paved driveway, their branches swaying in the early summer breeze, blocking the view of the house. All Maddie saw was the tall tower on the right with its large windows, the one in the middle made of stained glass. The tower was said to be the place where the two old women—presumed to be witches— created their potions and spells that kept little children away. No one went trick-or-treating at this house on Halloween. As a child, Maddie's parents had tried to take her down the drive-way to the brightly decorated house, but she'd cried until they gave up. Everyone knew if you walked into that house, you'd never come out.

"Silly childish stories," Maddie said aloud, still standing on the pavement. "There's no such thing as witches."

A squirrel dropped to the ground from a tree, and Maddie nearly jumped out of her skin.

Taking a deep breath, she forced herself to walk slowly down the driveway to the house.

It was all Caden's fault that Maddie was now taking her life in her hands at the haunted house. Caden Addams, her seventeen-year-old boyfriend who was wild and careless. He was the one who crashed Maddie's beloved red Toyota Corolla into a tree while driving recklessly on a dirt road in the woods. But then again, Maddie had let him, knowing full well that he wasn't careful with anything. She could never say no to him when he flashed his warm brown eyes at her or ran his hand through his thick, wavy brown hair. Caden was the boy every parent feared, and every teenage girl wanted to have as their boyfriend. And Maddie had been the lucky girl he'd chosen.

Now, she no longer felt so lucky.

"No car all summer," Maddie's father, Matthew Carlson, had proclaimed angrily. "It's going to sit at the repair shop until you pay for the repairs."

"But how will I make that kind of money?" Maddie had asked, tears running down her cheeks. "Working at the Frosty Freeze three nights a week will never earn enough to fix it."

"I guess you'll have to earn it another way," Matt had told her. "Caddie at the golf course. Work at Target. Mow lawns. Or better yet, make Caden pay for the damage. He wasn't supposed to be driving your car in the first place."

Maddie sighed. She knew her father was right. Owning the car had been a privilege, and she'd screwed it up. But Caden had no money, and his parents would never give him any. So, it was up to Maddie to pay for the repairs.

Target was out of the question because her mother, Sandy, would have to drive her to and from work. Even though her mother had summers off because she worked as a fourth-grade teacher all winter, Maddie didn't want to be seen being driven to her job by her mother. Being a caddie at their small-town country club wasn't a choice either. She'd be expected to work days and evenings, and she wanted to keep her Frosty Freeze job because it was perfect during the school year, too.

So, that left mowing.

Maddie's father had a driving lawn mower, which was necessary since each home in their neighborhood had at least two acres of land. He'd said she could use it, but she had to pay for the gas. Once school let out, Maddie walked around their neighborhood and the one adjacent to theirs, asking if anyone needed lawn mowing for the summer. Three people hired her, but it still wasn't enough to earn the money she needed.

"Did you ask Miss Arthur at the big house if she needed someone to mow?" Sandy casually asked Maddie one afternoon. "Their yard is twice as large as everyone else's."

Maddie frowned. "Miss Arthur?"

"Yes. The lady who owns the house you all say is haunted."

Maddie's brows rose. "I can't go there. They're witches."

Sandy laughed, smoothing back the brown strands that had fallen from her messy bun. "Sweetie. She's not a witch, and neither is the lady who lives there with her. They are nice older ladies who could use the help."

Maddie studied her mother for a moment. Her mother was forty-two and showed no sign of aging. Her skin was smooth, and she kept herself slim by running every day in the summer and using their treadmill all winter. Maybe her mother bought anti-aging potions from the old ladies. "How do you know them?" she asked suspiciously.

Sandy chuckled. "I just do. And they're harmless. It won't hurt you to ask if they need mowing done."

Maddie thought about that conversation as she forced her feet to take one step, and then another, down the long driveway. At seventeen, she was too old to believe in stories children made up on Halloween. She was sure the older women were harmless.

Her pounding heart told her otherwise.

As Maddie drew closer to the house, she saw that the land opened up around the big house. An expanse of lawn lay on each side and most likely went all the way to the back of the house and down to the lakefront. The house stood tall over Cedar Lake, the lake in their northern Minnesota town of Cedar Creek. Maddie had seen this house from the lakeside, and it looked even bigger with large glass windows and a deck that lined the entire front of the house. This was the first time she'd ever seen this side of the house, though.

The house stood on a hill, up from the driveway and garage. Stone steps led up to the front door, and large river rocks were laid about four feet tall, supporting three tiers of flower gardens on either side of the steps. The wood siding and hunter green trim on the windows were typical of an older lake home, but much to her surprise, the door was painted a deep orange. This made Maddie smile. The ladies couldn't be too scary if they had the good humor to paint their front door orange.

As she glanced around, she saw their lawn needed a good mowing. It was growing long, and weeds were trying to overtake the grass. The stone flower gardens held perennial flowering bushes, day lilies, and other plants, but they needed weeding, too. Maybe the ladies could use some help around this large house after all.

Taking a deep breath, Maddie climbed the stone steps. Halfway up, she jumped, startled by a garter snake sunning itself on the warm stone. The snake stuck out its tongue and slowly slithered away. Maddie cringed. She hated snakes.

Once at the door, she raised her hand and grasped the brass knocker. Hitting it twice against the brass plate beneath it, she waited for someone to answer. After what seemed like several minutes, Maddie heard footsteps walking to the door. It opened abruptly, and a tall woman with shining blue eyes stared at her.

"Well? What do you want?" the elderly woman asked bluntly.

Maddie stared at her, trying to regain her composure after the woman's demanding question. The elderly woman was tall, with curved shoulders. Her gray hair was cut short, and she wore turquoise earrings that swung from her ears when she moved. Her blue eyes bore into Maddie, waiting for an answer.

"Well?" the woman demanded.

"Hi. I'm sorry to bother you," Maddie said quickly. "I live in the neighborhood, and I wondered if you needed someone to mow your lawn this summer." She let out a breath after her fast, run-on sentence.

"Hm." The woman looked Maddie up and down. "So, you'd like to mow our lawn, would you?"

"Yes, ma'am," Maddie said, feeling the need to take a step back. The woman's eyes were narrowed as she scrutinized her. "If you don't already have someone to do it, that is."

"Hmph!" the woman snorted. "Does it look like we have someone mowing the lawn?"

Maddie was thinking of an answer when another elderly woman walked up behind the blunt one.

"Ginny. Who are you terrorizing?" A soft, lilting voice came from behind the first woman.

Ginny opened the door wider, and the other woman stepped

forward. Maddie nearly gasped. The woman was shorter than the first one but was trim and had perfect posture. She held a sleek cane in her slender hand, made of beautiful rosewood and topped with a gold-carved handle. The woman's silver hair was pulled up into a bun, and gold earrings hung from her ears. She was dressed in a long, flowing amethyst-colored blouse and a full skirt that fell below her knees. To Maddie, she looked like a graceful queen from a fairy tale.

"Oh, Eva. Let me have a little fun, would you?" the woman named Ginny said with a smirk. "This young lady was shaking in her sneakers. How can we continue our reputation as evil witches if we're nice to everyone?" She chuckled.

Eva shook her head and smiled. "Leave the girl be." She turned to Maddie. "What can we do for you, dear?"

"She wants to mow our lawn," Ginny answered for Maddie. "Do you really think this slip of a girl can mow our large yard?"

"Girls can do anything they set their minds to, Ginny. Now let her speak for herself," Eva said. Both women stared at Maddie expectantly.

Maddie looked first at Ginny, then at Eva (whom the other woman had pronounced as Ava). Were they sisters? She supposed they could be. But despite the one being rude and the other being sweet, they didn't seem as if they might boil and eat her.

"My father has a riding lawn mower I can use," Maddie said. "So, I could easily mow your lawn. I'm working for a few other people in the neighborhood if you'd like references."

Eva smiled, her blue eyes sparkling. "No need for references," she said. "Who did you say you were? Do you live in the neighborhood?"

"I'm Maddie Carlson. I live on the opposite side of the

street, about two houses down."

"Ah." Eva's face brightened. "You're Sandra's daughter."

"Yes," Maddie said, still wondering how her mother knew these ladies.

"I've known your mother since she was a girl. It would be nice to have her daughter helping us, wouldn't it, Ginny?" Eva said.

Ginny shrugged. "Can't be any worse than that boy we hired who never shows up." She turned to Maddie. "Will you show up?"

Maddie nodded. "Yes. I can mow as often as you need me to."

"Would you also weed trim around the rock walls and pull the weeds in our garden?" Eva asked. "As you can see, we are in no shape to do it ourselves."

"Speak for yourself," Ginny said haughtily.

Eva grinned.

"Yes, ma'am. I'd be happy to do those things also."

"Then you're hired," Eva said. "Would fifty dollars for each time you mow be enough? We'll add ten more when you weed trim and twenty more for weeding the garden."

Maddie's heart jumped. That would be more than enough. "Yes, that will be fine."

"When can you start?" Ginny asked. "We need someone to mow right away."

"I can start tomorrow," Maddie said. "As early as you'd like. I'd do it today, but I have to be at work at the Frosty Freeze by three this afternoon."

"Oh, you work there also?" Eva asked. "That's wonderful. You're an industrious young lady. Tomorrow is fine. Just not too early. I'm a bit of a night owl."

Ginny harrumphed again. "She stays up all night. It's a holdover from her stage days. Any time after nine is fine."

"Okay. I'll be here then. Thank you so much," Maddie said, smiling widely.

"See you tomorrow, dear," Eva said.

Maddie turned and walked down the stone steps. She was thrilled to have another mowing job, especially one that paid so well. Most of her other clients paid her twenty-five dollars each time. But then again, their yards weren't as large as the ladies' yard.

At least now she might actually earn enough to pay her parents back.

* * *

Two hours later, Maddie was behind the counter at the Frosty Freeze, tying her red and white striped apron over her jeans and T-shirt.

"I can't believe you actually knocked on the witches' door," Olivia Lang, Maddie's best friend since kindergarten, said. They both worked at the ice cream place, but didn't always have the same shift.

"They aren't witches," Maddie said, smiling at the next customer walking up to the counter. She took their order, and Olivia pulled two cones out to fill with ice cream. "They were very nice to me. Well, at least one was nice, and the other one was crabby."

"What did they look like?" Livie asked in a whisper as she handed the couple their cones. No one was waiting at the counter, so she gave her full attention to Maddie.

Maddie grinned at her friend. Livie was the complete

opposite of Maddie. While Maddie was tall with blond hair and blue eyes, Livie was shorter, with short dark hair and brown eyes. Livie was in great shape, though, since she'd been in gymnastics since she was five years old. She'd already won several local and state competitions and talked about working her way to the Olympics. But when it came to being a teenager, Livie was like every other teen, loving gossip and having a good time.

"They were older. Maybe in their eighties," Maddie said. "But they looked absolutely normal, like anyone's grandmother would look. Although," she hesitated, picked up a rag, and started wiping the stainless-steel countertop.

"Although what?" Livie asked, her eyes wide.

Maddie shrugged. "The one woman, Eva, was different from the other one. She looked regal, if that makes any sense. Her movements were graceful, even though she walked with a cane. And her voice was musical."

Livie blinked twice. "Well, that doesn't sound like a witch." She sounded disappointed. "Maybe she's your Fairy Godmother."

Maddie chuckled. She walked to the back room, brought out cups, and began refilling the cup holders. Then she took a clean rag and headed out to the small eating area to wipe the dirty tables. Maddie and Livie had been working there since they were fifteen. She knew the routine by heart and made sure her work was done well. The owners were nice to her, and she wanted to keep her job until she left for college.

"Hey, beautiful." Caden sauntered over to her in a dark T-shirt, ripped jeans, and worn work boots. He wore his boots summer and winter, except when they were lucky enough to go out on the lake with a friend whose family owned a boat.

"I'm working," Maddie said sternly, not looking at him. "Why aren't you working today?"

Caden ignored her brush-off and wrapped his arms around her. He was a good three inches taller and toned in all the right places for a seventeen-year-old. "I have the day off. Why don't you ditch this place, and we'll go to the lake and hang out?" He kissed her cheek, but Maddie pulled away.

"I'm working," she repeated. "I don't ditch my responsibilities." She started wiping the table harder than necessary, putting her full anger into it.

Caden sat on the table next to her. "Why aren't you any fun anymore?" he asked, running his hand through his wavy brown hair.

"Really?" Maddie stared straight at him. "Are you really going to ask me that? Have you forgotten you wrecked my car and now I have to pay to repair it?"

Caden laughed. "We were having fun that night. So, we banged into a tree. It's not like we got hurt or anything."

Maddie seethed. "You're lucky we didn't get hurt because my dad would have killed you. And I'm lucky I haven't been grounded until I graduate for letting you drive my car." Maddie stormed to the counter and tossed the dirty rag into the bin beneath.

Caden followed her, looking completely unscathed by her words. "How about a cone on the house?" he asked, leaning over the counter toward her. "Because I'm such a great kisser."

Maddie sighed. "Go away, Caden. I don't want to get into trouble here, too."

"Who's going to tell?" Caden asked. "It's only you and Livie here." He walked behind the counter, pulled a cone from the pop-up box, and filled it with vanilla soft serve. "See. That wasn't so hard, was it?"

"Caden, leave!" Maddie said.

He shrugged. "Okay. I'll see you after work."

"No, you won't. I have to go home after we close tonight," Maddie said. "I have a mowing job tomorrow, and I don't want to be late."

"Mowing? Yuck!" Caden said, licking his ice cream.

"She's mowing at the witches' house," Livie piped up. "She actually walked up to their door and lived to tell the tale."

"Really?" Caden looked impressed. "You mean they didn't try to eat you?"

"No, they didn't," Maddie said, irritated. "They were nice ladies. Now get out of here, Caden, before the owner drops by and sees you here."

He smiled, that drop-dead smile that always used to melt Maddie's heart. Now, she was becoming immune to it.

"Okay. See you later, beautiful." He sauntered out the same way he'd come in.

Livie sighed. "I know he's a bad boy, but I'm not sure I could be as angry at him as you are. He's so cute."

"If you were stuck mowing lawns all day, you'd be irritated, too," Maddie said. But she knew Livie was right. If Maddie had been truly angry with Caden, she would have pushed him away after the accident. Unfortunately, she still had trouble saying no to him.

A customer came in, and soon many more followed. Since the Frosty Freeze was across the street from the lake, it was always busy with tourists and locals out on their boats. Maddie was glad she was busy, though. It would make the day go faster. Then tomorrow, she'd be up early, mowing again.

No fun for her this summer. All because of Caden.

Chapter Two

Maddie

Maddie was up early the next day. She pulled her long hair up into a ponytail and dressed in a tank top and shorts. She figured if she was going to mow lawns, she might as well get a tan at the same time.

When she went downstairs for breakfast, all was quiet. Her father had already left for work, and her mother was gone on her morning run. Her younger sister, Lily, was still in bed. Maddie envied her. She wished she could lounge in bed until noon. But Lily was only twelve and was too young to have a boyfriend who got her into trouble. Maddie decided Lily was the lucky one.

After eating a protein bar and drinking a glass of milk, Maddie left a note on the counter saying she'd be out mowing. Then she went to the garage, opened the big door, and pushed the riding lawn mower outside before starting it. She also hooked the small trailer to the back so she could bring along the weed trimmer and a small cooler with water bottles.

The air was cool when she drove the mower down the quiet

neighborhood street toward the big house. It would get warmer as the day continued, and probably muggy as well. Being close to the water had its charms, but the humidity was the inevitable downside.

It was just nine o'clock when she pulled up to the driveway of the ladies' house. She detached the small trailer and pushed it into the ditch by the road, then sat on the mower. She started cutting the grass along the road and around the mailbox. Then she drove up one side of the driveway to the house. Turning, Maddie went down the other side of the driveway back out to the road. Once done, she attached the little trailer again and drove back up the driveway, leaving the trailer in the driveway while she began the task of mowing the larger sections of lawn.

As Maddie drove up and down the lawn on one side of the house, she saw a couple of lights on inside. From the driveway, the house looked like a regular ranch-style house with a big, tower-like addition on the right. But as she drove around to the other side, the blue lake appeared, and the land sloped gently toward the water. The house had a tall deck that ran the full length of the house, and the windows on the large addition were tall and wide. She wondered what that room was used for, and hoped she'd get a chance to see the inside someday.

Maddie spent two hours mowing the lawn all around the house because it hadn't been mowed for a while. She noted the cement patio adjacent to the walk-out basement door and the bricks surrounding the posts that supported the tall deck. The bricks held a pile of small stones beneath the deck, probably to absorb water that trickled down between the deck boards when it rained. She'd have to weed trim around those stones as well as around the cement patio. The job was much bigger than she'd first realized, but they were paying her well, so she had no complaints.

Maddie stopped the mower in the driveway just as the UPS truck appeared. The man handed her a package and backed the truck out. Maddie hadn't had a chance to tell him she didn't live there. Sighing, she walked up the stone steps, and as she was about to set the package on the porch, the door sprang open.

"Front door service!" Eva said with delight. "I can't tell you how difficult it is when they leave the packages at the bottom of the staircase."

Maddie smiled. Today, Eva wore a brightly colored flowered blouse with black pants and bright pink flats. Her earrings were pink stones set in gold, and her hair was up in a bun again. She looked like she was ready to go out for the day.

"I finished mowing," Maddie said. "I'm going to weed trim now."

"Oh, dear. You've been mowing all morning. Why don't you join us for an early lunch?" Eva asked. "Ginny was just making us grilled ham and cheese sandwiches."

Maddie wanted to say no, but Eva looked so hopeful to have company, she didn't have the heart to. "I'm a little dirty," she said.

"No problem. You've been working. Come in, dear." She moved aside with the use of her beautiful cane, then called out over her shoulder, "Ginny. We have company for lunch."

Ginny poked her head out of the kitchen. "Fine. If we must," she said.

Maddie quickly slipped off her sneakers and followed Eva inside. The entryway was actually a small living room with a stone fireplace and a sofa and chair. A bench sat by the door. The walls were painted a soft sage green, and beautiful canvas photographs of waterfalls and woodland areas in autumn hung on the walls.

"This is nice," Maddie said, glancing around.

"Thank you, dear," Eva said. "My mother lived here before I did, and she and my stepfather decorated it. But I like it, too."

Eva led her around the other way to where the kitchen opened to a small dining room. The kitchen had warm walnut cabinets and beautiful stone countertops. A sliding glass door led to the deck outside, and there was a lovely view of the lake.

"Would you like some iced tea?" Eva asked. "You must be thirsty after mowing for so long."

"Yes. Thank you," Maddie said. She felt awkward being inside the house. Ginny was across the kitchen near another door, making sandwiches on a griddle.

"So, we're to feed you, too?" Ginny asked grouchily. "We should dock your pay."

"Hush, Gin," Eva said. "Of course, we won't dock her pay. It's nice to have company for lunch."

Ginny complained under her breath while Eva used their refrigerator to pour ice into a tall glass, then took out a pitcher of tea to pour over it.

"Oh, let me carry that," Maddie said, rushing to Eva's side.

"Thank you, dear. It's awkward with the cane."

Maddie set the glass on the small oak table. "It's a pretty cane. I like the etchings on the gold handle."

"That's so kind of you, dear," Eva said, looking delighted. "An old friend of mine gave it to me years ago, and I used it for decoration. But now, I need it to walk." She sat at the table. "Do you see that the design is flowers and stems?" She handed the cane to Maddie.

Maddie sat down and held the cane in her hands. The

etchings were of flowers with long stems that entwined. "It's so beautiful," Maddie said. She handed it back to Eva.

"I saw it standing in the corner of my friend's apartment decades ago and mentioned how lovely it was. He smiled at me and told me I could have it. I was stunned," Eva said. "'Hopefully, I will never need it,' he told me in his thick Russian accent. I loved it so much, I kept it all these years."

Ginny glared at Eva as she set down a plate in front of her and then Maddie. "Nothing is ever free," she said.

"Oh, Gin." Eva sighed. "It was only a gesture of friendship."

Maddie felt uncomfortable, so she blurted out, "The sandwich looks delicious. Thank you for making it."

Ginny turned and looked at her. "Of course, it looks great. I made it." She returned to the table with her own sandwich and a plate of raw vegetables and dip. "Now eat up before it grows cold."

Maddie lifted one half of the sandwich and took a bite. It wasn't just a cheap cheese and cold cuts sandwich slapped together on the grill. The ham was fresh, and she couldn't quite make out what type of cheese it was. And there was some flavored mayonnaise on it. Whatever it was, it was delicious.

"Are you two ladies sisters?" Maddie asked, trying to make conversation.

"Humph. I should say not," Ginny said. "Do we look like sisters?"

"Well, um, yes," Maddie said.

Eva laughed. "We're cousins. And we do sort of look alike."

"Oh. That's interesting," Maddie said. "It's nice you can be together."

Ginny rolled her eyes and took another small bite of her sandwich.

"Tell me about your mother," Eva asked, barely touching her sandwich. "She's a teacher, isn't she?"

"Yes," Maddie said. "She teaches fourth grade. She likes working with younger children."

"And do you have any siblings?" Eva asked.

Maddie nodded. "Lily. She's twelve."

"How lovely," Eva said. "I always wished for a sister, but I was an only child."

"Hey. You had me," Ginny said.

"Not until we moved to New York, and by then you were busy with your friends and then interested in boys," Eva said.

"Well, you were always at the studio anyway. But I was still around," Ginny countered.

Maddie wondered what Ginny had meant by the "studio."

"I'll bet you have a handsome young man in your life," Eva said dreamily. "Is he the captain of the football team?"

Maddie laughed. "No, he's not. He's the opposite of that. And he's the reason I have to work all summer."

"Oh, my goodness. What did this young man do?" Eva asked.

"Don't be so nosey, Eva," Ginny said sternly. "You wouldn't want people asking you questions like that."

Eva's smile dropped. "Of course. That was rude of me. I'm sorry."

"It's okay," Maddie said, feeling bad for Eva. "I stupidly let him drive my car, and he crashed it into a tree. Now I have to earn enough to fix it. So, I'm mowing lawns and working as many shifts at the Frosty Freeze as possible, so I'll have my car back by fall for school."

Ginny shook her head. "Boys are trouble. They're always leaving messes for women to clean up." She looked up at

Maddie. "Why isn't that scoundrel paying for the repairs?"

Maddie wanted to laugh at the word 'scoundrel,' but Ginny was so serious that she didn't want to insult her. "He doesn't have much money and won't ask his parents."

"Well, I hope you dump him," Ginny said. "He won't ever amount to anything with that behavior."

"Now who's overstepping?" Eva said, looking at Ginny.

Ginny's lips tightened. "It's the truth, that's all."

"My dad would agree with you," Maddie said. "But it's hard for me to dump him. He's still important to me."

Eva reached over and patted Maddie's arm. "I understand completely."

"That's the truth," Ginny said, then looked regretful. "Sorry, Eva. You know what I mean."

"I do." Eva sighed.

Maddie finished her sandwich and tea and thanked the women profusely for lunch. "I'd better get back to weed trimming. Will it be okay if I weed the garden tomorrow? I have another lawn to mow this afternoon."

"That's fine, dear," Eva said. "Here. Let me pay you for mowing and trimming now in case you need to leave." She walked through the small living room and down a narrow hallway.

Ginny was stacking the dishwasher, so Maddie glanced around. She'd noticed the beautiful wood and glass pocket doors earlier that separated the smaller side of the house from the large tower room. They were long, and the stained glass depicted a lake with loons, blue herons, and swans on it. They were absolutely beautiful.

"My mother hired the stained-glass artist who created those panels," Eva said, coming up behind Maddie. "I just love them."

"They're beautiful. Is the big room on the other side?" Maddie asked.

Eva nodded. "But that is a story for another day." She handed Maddie her money. "Come visit us again after you work on the yard, and I'll show you the other side of the doors."

"Okay." She turned to Ginny. "Thanks again for lunch. It was delicious."

Ginny nodded and turned away.

"She hates compliments," Eva whispered. "I, however, love them." She smiled.

Everything about Eva filled Maddie with a warm feeling inside.

"I heard that," Ginny said.

Both Maddie and Eva laughed. Maddie headed to the door, then turned before leaving. "I'm glad I can work for you both," she said. "This has been fun."

"Me, too," Eva said. "See you tomorrow."

Maddie went down the stairs and finished trimming the lawn, feeling happier than she had in weeks.

* * *

That evening at dinner, Maddie mentioned eating lunch with the ladies. "They insisted I come inside and eat, and Ginny made the most delicious grilled sandwich," she told her parents and sister.

"Well, you're in a good mood," Matt said, smiling. "It's about time."

"They were nice to me," Maddie said.

"Even Mrs. Robertson?" Sandy asked, looking shocked. "She's always been a crab."

"Which one is Mrs. Robertson?" Maddie asked.

"Ginny."

"Oh, yeah. She's kind of grumpy. But the more she spoke, the more I realized she didn't mean it personally. She's the down-to-earth one of the two. I have a feeling Eva is the dreamer."

"Very astute," Sandy said.

"How do you know them, Mom?" Maddie asked. "Eva asked about you."

"Oh, it's a long story. Has she shown you the big room yet?" Sandy asked.

"No, but she said that was a story for another day."

Sandy smiled. "Well, that will explain a lot."

"I can't believe you're working for the scary witches," Lily piped up. "And you had lunch with them! Weren't you afraid they'd turn you into a frog?"

"They aren't witches," Sandy said to Lily. "Children make up those stories because the ladies are older. They're just regular people."

"And they're nice," Maddie said. "So don't pass those mean stories around. They aren't true."

Lily shrugged. "I'm still scared of them."

"Maybe you can come meet them sometime while I'm working," Maddie said.

Lily's eyes grew wide. "No way!"

Their parents laughed. As they finished dinner, a horn started honking outside their house.

Matt frowned as he rose with his empty plate in his hand. "Don't tell me. It's Caden."

Maddie went to the front window, looked out, and sighed. "I told him I didn't want to go out tonight." She went back to the table and started clearing it.

"Aren't you going outside to talk to him?" Sandy asked as they walked into the kitchen.

"He never listens. He can just sit out there."

Sandy grinned but knew better than to say anything.

The horn blasted again, making Maddie angrier. She pulled out her phone and texted Caden. *I'm not coming out. I told you I was staying home tonight.*

She brought more items into the kitchen from the table and put away the ketchup and bowl of salad after placing cling wrap over it. Her phone buzzed.

"Ah, come on. Let's go have some fun," Caden texted.

"No. Not tonight. I worked all day. You should try doing that once in a while," Maddie texted back.

"You can go out if you want to. I can finish up in here," Sandy told Maddie.

"I don't want to. I have some things I want to do tonight, and tomorrow I have another full day of work."

"Your choice," Sandy said.

A knock came on the kitchen door. Maddie looked up and saw Caden through the door's small window. She stormed to the door and opened it. "Why are you here? I told you I didn't want to go out tonight."

He took a step back as if she'd hit him. "We never go out anymore," he said. "Don't you want to do something fun?"

Maddie looked over her shoulder at her mother working at the sink, then pushed Caden out of the way. She walked outside and closed the door. "I don't get to have fun anymore, remember? I work most days and then evenings at the Freeze. All because of you."

Caden rolled his eyes. "That's all I ever hear you say anymore."

He drew closer and wrapped his arms around her. "Don't you miss spending time alone together? I do."

Maddie stepped back, and his arms dropped. "You hear me say I work all the time because that's what I do. If you helped pay for the damage, I wouldn't have to work so hard. I'm staying home tonight."

"Fine," Caden said, growing angry. "But don't be surprised if I find a new friend to hang out with."

"Go ahead," Maddie said. "You can trash her car, too."

Caden's anger abated. "I don't want a new girlfriend. I want you," he said softly. "Can we go out tomorrow night?"

"I work at the Freeze tomorrow until closing," Maddie said.

"Then the next night, okay? We can go to that new Marvel movie."

Maddie felt her energy fading. She was exhausted, and tired of fighting with Caden. "Fine. We'll go to the movie."

Caden smiled. "Great. I'll pick you up at six-thirty." He moved closer to kiss her, but Maddie put her hand on his chest.

"My mom can see us. I'll see you later, okay?"

Caden sighed. "Okay." He turned and walked around to the front of the house to leave.

Maddie headed back inside and saw her mother had already stacked the dishwasher and cleared off the table. "I'm going up to my room," she said.

"Okay."

Once in her room, Maddie grabbed a notebook and dropped onto her bed. Ever since she'd spoken to the ladies today, she'd wanted to write down everything they'd said in her notebook.

Maddie liked to write. She was the odd one in English class who was thrilled when the teacher said to write a thousand-word story about anything. She kept a diary of sorts, but it was just a notebook that she wrote in about the things she did that day or the conversations she'd had. She had five filled notebooks stacked up in her closet, and this one was already half full.

She'd already written about the first day she'd met Eva and Ginny. She'd written how scared she'd been walking up the long driveway, and how she'd felt climbing the stairs and knocking on the door. And then how happy she was that they'd hired her. Sitting back against her thick bed pillows, she grabbed her favorite pen off her nightstand and started.

Maddie had a feeling she'd be writing a lot about the ladies in the big house.

CHAPTER THREE

Maddie

Maddie arrived at the ladies' house at nine the next morning and began weeding the three-tiered rock garden that lay on both sides of the front door. Each tier was about three feet tall and six feet long. From what Maddie could tell, they hadn't been weeded for quite a while.

Wearing gloves, she pulled the weeds and dropped them into a garbage bag. She had to be careful not to step on the flowers popping out of the ground or the bushes that filled large spaces. A garter snake slithered past her as she reached for a weed, and she nearly fell backward off the wall. Maddie didn't mind mice or chipmunks, but she hated snakes.

The day grew warmer as she worked. She'd brought along a cooler with water, anticipating that the weather would turn hot. After she was done here, she could go home, shower, and then head to her shift at the Frosty Freeze.

After an hour and a half of weeding, the garden looked nice. Maddie wasn't sure what the ladies did about garbage—if they had pick-up once a week or someone took it to the dump for them—so she decided to ask. She climbed the steps to the front door and knocked.

The door opened quickly, and Ginny stared back at her. "Are you finished already?" she asked, looking past Maddie to inspect the gardens.

"Yes," Maddie said. "Do you have a garbage bin I can put the bag of weeds in?"

"There's a big one in the garage. The neighbor rolls it up the driveway for us each week and then rolls it back. I'll hit the button for you." Ginny walked to a side table in the small living room and opened a drawer. She pulled out a control and pressed the button. The garage door opened.

"Thank you," Maddie said.

"Here. Let me give you money before you go down. No sense in wasting energy walking down and then up again."

Maddie waited while Ginny disappeared, then returned. "Here's for the weeding. If it doesn't rain much this week, you can probably wait until next week to mow again."

"Okay. Thank you." Maddie glanced past Ginny, looking for Eva, but she wasn't around.

"Eva is resting," Ginny said, as if reading her mind. "She tires easily sometimes. But she'll be fine."

"Oh. Okay." Maddie was disappointed that Eva wasn't there to talk. "I hope she feels better soon. Thanks again. I'll see you next week."

Ginny nodded and closed the door.

Maddie went home and placed her earnings in the desk drawer in her bedroom. Even though her car had insurance, it hadn't been covered for Caden driving it, so it didn't cover the accident. That was why her parents were making her pay for it—along with the fact that they'd told her never to let any of her friends drive her car. So, she'd been saving her money in her desk drawer for when the repair shop was finished with it. Maddie knew it was going to cost a lot, so she hoped she earned enough to cover it.

She showered and ate lunch, then borrowed her mother's car to drive to work. Her dad was still at work, and her mom had driven Lily to gymnastics in the red Jeep. The Jeep was fun to drive, but her father wouldn't let her use it.

When she arrived at work, Maddie was disappointed to see that Livie wasn't working with her. Instead, an older girl, Carrie, who attended college in town, was there. Carrie was tall and thin with long dark hair and was twenty years old. All she ever talked about was how she was going to make so much money after she graduated from college. Maddie didn't know what her major was and didn't care. So, they basically worked in silence.

Business that day was slow, so Maddie made several runs to the back room to restock supplies. On one run when she returned, Caden was behind the counter making himself an ice cream cone while Carrie stood glaring at him with her arms crossed.

"Tell her it's okay if I grab a cone," Caden told Maddie. "I do it all the time."

"It's not okay," Carrie said. "And he has to pay for it."

Maddie turned on Caden. "I've told you a thousand times you can't do that. Will you listen to me for once?"

"Aw, babe. You can't stay angry with me," Caden said, licking his cone. "Besides. I don't have any extra money to pay for it."

Carrie continued glaring at them.

"I'll pay for it," Maddie told Carrie.

"Fine. But I'd better not see him doing that again, or I'm telling the owners." Carrie stormed over to the drive-up window just as a car rolled up.

"Caden! Are you trying to get me fired? I have to work. Leave."

"If you were fired, we could spend more time together," Caden said, grinning.

"No, we wouldn't," Maddie said, seething. "I'd have to find another job to pay my parents back. And it probably won't be as flexible as this one." Maddie let out a breath. "Just go."

Caden grew serious. "You think I don't understand how serious it was that I crashed your car. I do. And if I had the money to fix it, I'd give it to you. But you know what my family's like. The money I make at the car wash is all I have to buy the stuff I need. My parents don't buy groceries for me and my younger brother—I do. I'm the one who makes sure he eats and has clothes that fit. I'm the one who drives him to school every day. I'm sorry I can't help you, but that's why."

Maddie's heart melted. "I had no idea," she said softly. "You've never told me this before."

"I didn't want you to feel sorry for me," he said. "Or look at me the way you are right now. I'm supposed to be tough Caden. Not someone to pity." He turned to leave. "I'll see you later."

Maddie followed him to the door. "Caden."

He turned. "What?"

She was at a loss for words. She didn't want him to think she felt bad for him because she knew he hated it. "We're still on for Friday night, right?"

He smiled. "Yes. I'll come get you at six thirty." He left, hopping up into his beat-up pickup and driving away.

As Maddie watched him, she finally realized why he always wore his beat-up boots and jacket, and why he didn't fix up his truck. All his money went to taking care of his little brother.

Her heart ached for him.

That night, as she sat in her princess-style bedroom with white furniture, a thick white-and-pink comforter, and a closet full of clothes and shoes, it hit Maddie just how spoiled she was. No wonder her parents were making her pay for the car repairs. They had bought the used car for her sixteenth birthday, but had warned her that it could easily be taken away if she misused it. They even bought her gas. Her checks at the Frosty Freeze used to be for her to buy clothes and anything else she wanted. Caden didn't have a family life like that. She knew he'd saved for a year to buy his truck at the junk yard for five hundred dollars, and his uncle helped him get it running. At the time, she'd thought it was a guy thing to have a beat-up truck. Now, she knew differently.

Pulling her notebook out of the nightstand drawer, Maddie began to write what had happened that day. She mentioned that Eva hadn't felt well and how she hoped she'd feel better soon. She wrote about her conversation with Caden at the Freeze. And her realization of how much she took her family and their nice life for granted.

The next day, Maddie didn't have to mow lawns or work at the Freeze, so she slept in, then picked up her room and hung out with Lily for a while. She tried calling Livie to see if she wanted to hang out, but her friend didn't answer. So, she asked Lily if she wanted to go to the neighbor's house across the street and swim in the lake.

"You never have time for me," Lily said, clutching her towel under her arm. They both had swimsuits on with T-shirts over them and flip-flops. "Why today?"

Maddie chuckled. "Why not today?"

They knocked on the neighbor's door first to let them know they were using their beach, but there was no answer. So, they walked around the side of the house and headed down to the small, sandy beach. They had an open invitation from the neighbor to use their beach anytime they wanted. So, it didn't feel odd being in their yard when they weren't home.

Both girls were strong swimmers, but Maddie still kept an eye on Lily as she swam out into the lake and back. It was early summer, so the water was still cold, but it felt good. Maddie only waded in because she didn't want to get her hair wet, but that all went south when Lily and she got into a splashing fight and both were drenched. Afterward, they lay on their towels on the beach and dried off in the sun.

"I'm glad you asked me to do this," Lily said, turning her face toward Maddie as they lay there. "We never do anything together anymore. You're either working or out with Caden." She said Caden like it was a dirty word.

"Well, I'm older than you. That means I'm busier, that's all," Maddie said.

"Why do you date that guy anyway?" Lily asked. "Even his brother thinks he's a jerk."

Maddie frowned. She lifted herself on her elbows and stared at Lily. "Do you know Caden's younger brother?"

"Well, yeah. Duh! We're in the same grade. And it's not like our town is that big."

"Why does he think Caden's a jerk?" Maddie asked. She had a bad feeling in the pit of her stomach.

"Alex says Caden is always bullying him. He punches him and takes his stuff. On Alex's birthday last spring, he got twenty-five dollars from his grandparents, and Caden stole it. He didn't dare tell his parents because Caden's always in trouble at home, and he didn't want to make it worse."

Maddie was stunned. Caden stole his brother's birthday money? That was awful. "Does Alex always have lunch money for school?" Maddie asked. "And does he seem to wear the same clothes all the time like Caden does?"

Lily turned her head and pulled down her sunglasses. "Of course, Alex has money to buy lunch every day," she said. "And he never wears old clothes. He's kind of fussy about his clothes and backpack and stuff. One day, a kid stepped on his sneakers and got them dirty, and Alex had a fit." Lily stared at her. "Why are you asking all of this?"

"It's just something Caden told me yesterday, that's all," Maddie said. She lay back, and so did Lily.

"Have you ever been to Caden's house?" Lily asked.

"No. He said his parents hate it when his friends come over."

"Weird," Lily said. "I mean, you two have been dating for over a year, and he's been to our house a million times."

Maddie agreed. But she kept silent. Instead of relaxing on the beach, she was stewing over being lied to by Caden.

That night, Maddie grabbed a quick sandwich instead of eating dinner with the family.

"What are you doing tonight?" her father asked.

"I'm going to a movie with Caden," she said, knowing her father wouldn't like hearing that.

"Oh. Well, I hope he at least pays for that," Matt said.

"Dad!"

Matt shrugged.

Maddie pulled a Diet Coke from the refrigerator. "Dad?

Do you know where Caden's dad works?"

"Yeah. He's a county surveyor," Matt said. "Good job with great benefits."

"Really?" Maddie was shocked. She'd thought Caden's dad didn't earn a good living.

Sandy came into the kitchen. "What are you talking about?"

"Caden's dad," Matt said. "Maddie wanted to know where he worked."

"Oh." Sandy checked their dinner cooking in the stove. "His mom works as a counselor at the college. She's nice, but I don't know her that well. We say hi at the grocery store once in a while."

Maddie's eyes widened. "You've seen Caden's mom in the grocery store?"

"Sure, honey. She has two growing boys to feed. I'm sure their grocery store bill is huge." Sandy chuckled.

A loud honk came from outside the house.

"Sheesh, Maddie. That's so annoying," Matt said. "Why can't he come get you at the door like a human being?"

"Because he knows you don't like him," Maddie said. "I'll be at the movies." She picked her phone and small bag up off the counter and headed outside. She and Caden had to talk.

"My dad hates it when you honk. You're supposed to come to the door," Maddie said the moment she hopped into Caden's truck.

He stared at her. "Are you kidding? Your dad hates me."

"That's what I told him," Maddie said. "But from now on, no more honking. If you want to see me, you have to come knock on the door."

Caden put his truck in reverse and pulled out of the drive-way. "Cripes. You'd think we were living in the 1950s."

Maddie was silent as they drove across town to the movie theater. She wanted to confront Caden about the obvious lies he'd told her yesterday. But she wasn't sure how to say it. Caden turned up the music on the radio, which prevented Maddie from speaking.

They pulled into the parking lot, which was full, and Maddie was surprised when Caden drove around the building to the back, where the employees parked.

"Why are we back here?" Maddie asked.

"Come on. Let's go," Caden said, jumping out of the truck and completely ignoring her question.

He grabbed her hand and pulled her toward the back door.

"Caden! Why are we back here?" Maddie asked again.

Caden knocked on the door. "My cousin, Rudy, works here. He said he'd get us in for free."

"What?" Maddie was stunned. "You won't even pay for us to see a movie?"

Caden looked confused. "Why pay when you can get in for free?"

The door opened, and a tall, gangly kid with a mop of red hair waved them inside. Caden grabbed Maddie's hand again and pulled her inside with him.

"Thanks, Rudy," Caden said. "I owe you one."

Rudy looked nervous. "If I get caught, you'll owe me more than one," he said. "Go right to the theater and don't go up front. They check your ticket stub if you go into the lobby and try to get back to the movie."

Caden laughed. "I'll just say I lost it."

Rudy stared hard at him. "No. Just go watch the movie." He headed off down the hallway.

Maddie followed Caden as they walked to theater number

five, where the Marvel movie was playing. They were early, so there weren't many people sitting in there. They chose seats up near the back in the middle.

"It's the best place to see and hear the movie," Caden said, as if he were an expert.

"We have to talk," Maddie said, turning to look at Caden. "This is too much. It's like stealing. Like when you take ice cream for free at the Freeze. It's wrong."

"Oh, come on, Mads," Caden said in his sweet boyfriend voice. "I'm just saving a little money. We're not hurting anyone."

"You never used to be like this," Maddie said. "You paid for our movies before, and even if we stopped for a burger somewhere. Now, you're always scheming."

"I told you yesterday why I never have any money," Caden said, widening his eyes.

"Don't give me that puppy-dog look," Maddie said. "You lied to me yesterday. I know your dad and mom both have good jobs. And your brother isn't starving."

Caden sat back deep in his seat. "Okay. Yeah. I exaggerated a little. But I do drive Alex to school every day because my mom has to be at work early, and the bus doesn't come out to our house."

"Caden! Why would you lie to me?"

"Because you were so mad. And I hate when you're mad at me. Like now. Can't we relax and enjoy the movie?" Caden reached out to place his arm around Maddie, but she pushed him away.

"I'm not staying," Maddie said, standing up.

"Why?" Caden looked surprised. "We're here. Do you want a soda or something? I can go get you one."

"God, Caden! You just don't get it, do you? Have you always

acted this way, and I didn't see it? Because it feels like you've changed. A lot," Maddie said.

Caden sat back in his chair again. "I haven't changed. You have. You take everything too seriously, Mads. You need to chill out."

Maddie's heart pounded with rage. How could she ever have thought she loved this guy? As the theater darkened and the previews began, Maddie walked down the steps and headed out of the theater. When she saw that Caden didn't follow her, she went to the lobby and texted Livie.

"Can you pick me up at the theater and take me home?"

"Sure. I'll be right there," Livie responded.

Maddie walked outside, sat on a bench, and waited.

Chapter Four

Maddie

The next few days, Maddie was happy to be busy working, so it took her mind off Caden. He really was a jerk. After Livie picked her up, Maddie had ranted about all the things Caden had done until tears started to flow. Livie had pulled over into the McDonald's parking lot and reached for her friend's hand.

"Sorry he's been such a jerk," Livie told her. "I've never had to deal with a boyfriend, so I'm not much help."

"It's okay," Maddie said, wiping tears from her eyes. "I don't know if I'm mad at him or at myself for putting up with his crap. I feel like a loser."

"You, Maddie, are not the loser in this scenario. That much I know for sure," Livie said. "Let's go through the drive-up and get ice cream. It'll help."

Maddie did feel better after they'd both sat in the car and eaten ice cream. Something about spending time with her closest friend and eating ice cream was soothing.

She mowed lawns and worked at the Frosty Freeze all week, putting all her energy into work. Caden did try to call and texted he was sorry, but Maddie ignored him. She wasn't sure if she wanted to be around him anymore. He was too immature.

On Thursday morning, Maddie went to Eva and Ginny's house to check their lawn and was surprised at how tall it had grown. It had rained, and they'd had warm weather, so it had grown quickly. Maddie went back to her house, got the mower, and drove it down the driveway. She wanted to ask the ladies first before mowing. They were paying her well, and she didn't want to take advantage of them.

When she knocked on the door, Ginny answered.

"Oh, hi," Ginny said in a monotone voice as if she was disappointed it was Maddie at her door. "Are you going to mow today?"

"I wanted to ask first, to make sure you wanted it done today," Maddie said. She always felt uncomfortable talking to Ginny.

"Yes. Of course. It's getting long," Ginny said. "I suppose you'll want to eat lunch with us, too."

"Uh, no. I appreciated it last week, but you don't have to feed me," Maddie said.

"Well, come in around eleven-thirty," Ginny said. "Eva will insist on you having lunch." She closed the door, leaving Maddie standing there. Sighing, Maddie went down to the mower and began working.

Mowing took a while in their large yard. There were also many trees on the lakeside that she had to mow around. It was mindless work, giving Maddie time to stew over Caden. She couldn't understand why he was being such a jerk. Ever since the car accident, he'd been different. Or at least, she thought he was different. Maybe she was the one changing.

When they'd first started dating a year ago, he'd been sweet and attentive. Considering he'd had a "bad boy" reputation, Maddie hadn't seen him that way. They'd had fun on dates and spent time with their friends. But slowly, things changed. She just had no idea why.

After finishing the lawn, Maddie walked up the steps to the house. It wasn't quite eleven thirty, but she didn't plan on staying for lunch anyway. She didn't want to impose on the women.

"Oh, Maddie! You're here." Eva answered the door before Maddie even knocked and had a broad smile on her sweet face. "I do hope you'll join us for lunch. I love having the company."

"That's so kind of you," Maddie said. "But I don't want to be any trouble."

"Trouble? Why, you're far from trouble," Eva said, moving aside to let her in.

Today she wore black pants and a black T-shirt, with a colorful, kimono-style jacket that floated around her. Her earrings had tiny amethyst stones hanging down her neck, capturing the amethyst in her jacket.

"Says the lady who's not cooking lunch," Ginny huffed from the kitchen.

Eva laughed. "Don't listen to her. She loves company, too."

Reluctantly, Maddie slipped off her sneakers and followed Eva around the corner to the table by the beautiful pocket doors. Maddie gazed at the doors, still curious about what lay behind them.

Eva smiled. "Would you like to see what is so mysterious behind those doors?"

Maddie's heart pounded with excitement. "Yes. I'd love to see what the room looks like."

"Don't slide those doors yourself," Ginny ordered, stopping

what she was doing and wiping her hands on a towel. She walked over and placed her hand in an indented metal handle on one side while Eva did the same on the other. They pulled the doors in opposite directions. Immediately, light filled the small dining room as Maddie gazed into the big, open space.

"Oh, my goodness," Maddie said, stepping into the sundrenched room, feeling like Alice entering Wonderland. Her mind immediately registered what she saw, and she turned to Eva. "You taught ballet?"

Eva stepped into the room beside her while Ginny shook her head and headed back into the kitchen. "Yes, dear. I taught ballet in this room for years."

Maddie looked all around her, taking in every detail. The room was twice as tall as the rest of the house with a peaked ceiling. On the left were the floor-to-ceiling windows that faced the lake. On the right were French doors. Straight ahead, the wall held a large, stone fireplace with a wood mantel. The wood floor was a light honey color, and along the sides of the room were portable ballet barres, placed to maximize the number of students. But the most amazing feature of all were the tall, black-and-white photos around the room depicting a young woman in various ballet poses.

"Are these photos of you?" Maddie asked in wonder, walking across the room to one large photo.

"Yes, they are," Eva said. "I was in my twenties. It seems rather obnoxious to have pictures of yourself all around the room, but my mother thought it would give legitimacy to the dance studio and to me as a teacher."

"That's a beautiful arabesque," Maddie said, turning back to Eva. "Your form was perfect."

Eva's brows shot up. "You know ballet?"

Maddie smiled as she walked over to another portrait of Eva performing a perfect jump. "Only a little. I took a few years of ballet when I was a child, but I gave it up. It wasn't really for me. But I know a good stance when I see it."

Eva walked over to Maddie. "That one was taken while I performed *Symphony in C* with the New York City Ballet."

Maddie turned and stared at Eva, completely stunned. "You danced for that company?"

Eva nodded. "Yes. A long time ago. But before any of that. First, there was the school."

CHAPTER FIVE

Eva – 1947

Little Eve Arthur didn't remember much about her childhood until after her fourth birthday. All she knew was that her mother worked hard to keep a roof over their heads and that her father was not in the picture. By the time Eve turned five, her mother decided to enroll her in a dance class, because the little girl loved jumping and twirling around their tiny apartment.

"You shouldn't waste your hard-earned money on dance classes," their well-meaning older neighbor, Martha Kranski, told Eve's mother, Gwendelyn. Mrs. Kranski babysat little Eve while Gwen worked as a maid in the lovely homes in Beverly Hills.

"It's not a waste if it's for my little Eve," Gwen told the elderly woman. "I want her to have everything I didn't."

Mrs. Kranski snorted and huffed, but she had no say in the matter. She did adore little Eve, and it seemed like the little girl had a natural talent.

Eve's mother had been raised in the Bronx, New York, by hard-working parents who were always trying to scrape together enough money to pay the rent. So, she understood the value of hard work and was determined to better herself. At nineteen, she married Joel Arthur, who dreamed big but didn't back it up with work. After Eve was born, he moved the family to Southern California, believing that the opportunities were better out there. But as the draft for WWII came calling, Joel hightailed it to Mexico so he wouldn't have to fight, deserting Gwen and Eve.

Not willing to hitch her wagon to another man, Gwen worked days as a maid and went to night school to learn secretarial skills to better herself. She knew she was capable of doing better for herself and little Eve. Paying for dance lessons was worth every penny.

Like her mother, Eve was a dreamer. She loved the freedom of running, twirling, and jumping around the dance studio, but as she grew older, she also learned to appreciate the discipline required to execute the steps needed to perform. Her first two ballet teachers were young women who let the girls enjoy their classes. But then she moved up to the more serious class, where an older woman with a thick Russian accent demanded they start learning. While the other seven and eight-year-olds complained or quit, Eve loved the class. As the elderly dance instructor tapped her cane on the wooden floor to the time of the music, Eve would plié, relevé, and echappé at the barre, keeping time with the thump, thump, thump of the teacher's cane. A gentleman played songs on the piano for the girls to follow the beat, but it was the clicking of the cane that Eve found easy to follow.

By the time Eve was nine, she was pirouetting and leaping grand jetés across the floor with ease, and Madame Sokolova paid particular attention to her training. One day after class, she asked Eve to wait.

"Why do you take dance lessons?" Mme Sokolova asked Eve.

The little girl in the black leotard and pink tights stared up at her, confused. "Because I love to dance?"

"But do you love to dance, or do you have to dance?" the elderly teacher asked.

Eve thought about the question. To her young mind, they both seemed the same. "I have to dance," she replied. "I've always wanted to dance, and I hope to dance forever."

Mme Sokolova smiled and nodded. "Wonderful, child. You may go."

Eve left, feeling confused, but also feeling like she'd said the right thing. At least Mme Sokolova smiled at her answer, and a smile from her was rare.

Several months later, Mme Sokolova approached Gwen about Eve's future.

"There is a ballet school in New York City that Eve should audition for. If she is serious about dance, this is the school she should attend," Mme Sokolova told her. The Russian teacher knew what she spoke of. She'd left the Soviet Union years ago via Paris, France, and along the way, had danced with several prestigious dance companies. The man who now ran the dance studio and choreographed for the New York City Ballet was someone she'd danced with. Mme Sokolova knew that Eve had the ability to dance for him.

Gwen took the teacher's recommendation seriously. She still had a sister who lived in New York, so it was possible to return there to live.

"Would you like to try out for the dance school in New York?" Gwen asked Eve. "If they accept you, it will mean hard work and dedicating your life for the next few years to ballet."

"And we'd have to move to New York?" Eve asked. The thought of living in such a big city both frightened and intrigued her.

Gwen nodded. "If we move, we'll stay, even if you aren't accepted into the school. But if that happens, we'll just find another school for you."

Even at ten, Eve knew that uprooting their lives for a dream was a big deal. And the fact that her mother was willing was even more spectacular. "I'd like to try," she said.

Gwen nodded. "Then we're off to New York City!"

Mme Sokolova told Eve she'd send a letter of recommendation to the School of American Ballet for her. This would at least get Eve's foot in the door. Eve and her mother quickly packed up their small apartment, leaving all the furniture behind.

"We'll only take what we can carry on the train," Gwen told her.

Eve packed everything she held dear, most of it being her ballet clothes and dance shoes. She had two stuffed animals from her childhood that she loved dearly, and packed them into her suitcase. That was all she really needed. If she were going to make dancing her life, she'd have to learn to pack light.

After saying their goodbyes to Mrs. Kransky and their other neighbors, they boarded a train that would take them across the country to New York City. For Eve, it was an entirely new experience. For Gwen, it meant going home.

Gwen's older sister, Beatrice, and her husband, Roger Crandell, met the pair at the train station. The two women hugged while Roger carried their luggage to the car.

"And this is our little ballerina!" Bea said, hugging Eve tightly. "We're so excited to have you both at our house. My Ginny is your age, and you two will have such fun together."

"Thank you so much for letting us stay. I hope we won't be in your way," Gwen told her sister.

"We have plenty of room. It's no problem," Bea told her.

When they arrived at the Crandells' apartment, both Gwen and Eve were surprised at how much room they had. The apartment had a doorman, and they lived on the fifth floor. There were four bedrooms, two bathrooms, a large living and dining room, a modern kitchen, and even a small den that Roger used as a library and office. Compared to the one-room apartments Eve had grown up in, this place was a palace.

"So much space," Gwen said, looking all around her. "And such beautiful furnishings."

"Thank you," Bea said, beaming. "Roger is doing quite well at the advertising agency. He just became a partner."

Gwen was impressed, and it took a lot to impress her.

A young girl with pigtails came to greet them, along with a small boy with dark hair and eyes.

"This is Ginny and Norman," Bea said to Gwen and Eve. "They're excited to have a cousin staying with us."

Ginny walked right up to Eve and looked her up and down. "You're shorter than I am," she said. "I thought we were the same age."

Eve stared at Ginny, stunned that she would say such a thing. "My ballet teacher says being petite will help me with my dance career."

Ginny grinned and grabbed Eve's hand. "Come on. I'll show you our room." She pulled her down the long hallway and into a nice-sized bedroom with twin beds and puffy pink quilts.

"I hope you like pink," Ginny said, shaking her head. "My mother thinks all girls should have pink and white rooms. Ugh! I'd prefer blue."

"I think it's beautiful," Eve said, mesmerized by how lovely everything was.

"I made room in my closet for your clothes. But if you need more space, you can keep things in the guest room," Ginny said in a take-charge manner.

"Oh." Eve stared at her small bag of clothes. "I won't need much room. I mostly have dance clothes and a couple of nice dresses."

"That's it?" Ginny looked shocked. "I might have some dresses I've outgrown that would fit you." Ginny began digging through her closet. "You will definitely need more clothes for when you start school."

"My mom said that if I'm accepted into the dance school, I'll attend the Professional Children's School. That way I'll have more time for practice," Eve said.

Ginny stared at her. "You really take this ballet stuff seriously, don't you?"

Eve laughed. "Yes. I do."

After Gwen and Eve were settled into their new home, Gwen immediately scoured the papers for a job. She was going to use her newly learned secretarial skills to try to find a job. She appreciated her sister's generosity in offering her a home, but knew she'd need to find her own apartment soon. Plus, there was the cost of attending the School of American Ballet. Gwen knew it wasn't cheap and hoped they could apply for a scholarship if Eve were accepted.

A week after arriving, the day of Eve's audition came. On the eight-block walk from the apartment to the dance studio,

Gwen and Eve talked about what her professional dancer's name should be.

"Eve Arthur is too plain," Gwen said. "You need a ballerina name."

"But I like my name," Eve said.

"Yes, but we need a fancy name." Gwen thought. "What about Evalina Ashford? People can call you Eva for short."

"It is fancy," Eve said. "But Ashford isn't my last name."

"No. But you can have a stage name. Just think about it," Gwen said.

They arrived at the building on East 59th Street and opened the door. A long staircase stared back at them, so they walked up all twenty-nine steps and opened the door at the top. A long, narrow hallway with multiple doors greeted them. Music played from inside one of the many rooms down the hallway. An older woman in a nice suit came out of a door and stood behind the desk.

"May I help you?" she asked.

"Eve Arthur is here for her audition," Gwen said.

The woman looked at a sheet of paper on top of the desk. "Oh, yes. Do you have your dance clothes with you?"

"Yes. Under my dress," Eve said. "And I have my dance slippers, too."

The woman smiled. "Good. Go into the room behind you and get ready. I see your hair is already up, which is perfect. Then I'll take you to practice."

Eve quickly changed and brought her bag of clothes out to her mother. The lady smiled again. "Come along. You'll work with the class in progress so we can see what level you are."

Eve glanced at her mother for approval, and she nodded her head. Then Eva followed the woman down the hallway. When the door opened, the music poured out into the hallway. Young girls were at the barre, their steps following along to the music provided by a woman on the piano.

"Just find a spot and follow along. Do the best you know how," the woman said.

Eve spotted an open space across the room and quietly hurried to it. She took her stance in fifth position as the other girls had and began following along. They were performing simple steps, pliés, relevés, echappés, and grand pliés in first, second, and fifth positions. She followed along, keeping her back straight as she'd been taught, her arm extended with the elbow up and the hand loose.

Each time they finished an exercise, they'd turn in unison and begin the same exercise on the other side. Eve kept her mind on the music and following the other girls. It wasn't until she'd turned again that she saw a slim man with hollow cheeks and his hair combed back standing beside the teacher and watching. His dark eyes were on her.

Trying not to be nervous, Eve kept her mind on the music and movements until the barre part of the class was over. All the girls found a place on the floor to stretch, and Eve did also. Then they started the center work. Jumps, pirouettes, and other movements were done from corner to corner on the hardwood floor. This was Eve's favorite part of class. She extended her legs with ease while jumping high in the air, something the other girls hadn't mastered yet. After class, one girl came up to her.

"Are you new here?" the pretty girl with the blond ponytail asked.

"I hope to be," Eve said.

"You're sure to be invited here with those jumps," the girl said.

Eve remembered to thank the teacher as she left the room and then forced herself not to run down the hallway to tell her mother how she had done. But as she neared her mother, she saw the same man from the classroom talking to Gwen. Eve slowed her steps, not sure if she should approach.

"Eve. Come along," Gwen said, waving to her.

Eve walked up to her mother and the man. Now that she was closer to him, she saw he had a kind face, even when he looked serious.

"We were just discussing your future with this school," Gwen said, smiling at the gentleman. "This is Mr. Balanchine."

Eve looked up into the man's dark eyes. She knew who George Balanchine was and also knew that he had the last say about who attended his school. "It's nice to meet you, Mr. Balanchine," she said, her voice shaking.

He smiled. "Very nice to meet you, Eve. I see you have worked hard and learned well. Would you like to start classes at our little school?"

"Oh, yes," Eve said excitedly. "I would."

"Wonderful. Work hard and make us proud," Mr. Balanchine said. He looked over at Gwen. "And we will send you the paperwork so Eve can get started."

"Thank you, Mr. Balanchine," Gwen said, her eyes beaming.

Eve turned to her mother. "Have I been accepted?"

"Oh, yes, dear. You have. And Mr. Balanchine has also offered you a full scholarship, so we can afford to send you. Isn't that exciting!"

Eve was relieved and excited all at once. She was finally going to be working toward her dream.

CHAPTER SIX

Maddie

"George Balanchine? You studied at his dance school?" Maddie asked, stunned. "That's amazing."

Eva smiled warmly. "I'm glad to see you know who he was. Mr. B, that's what we all called him, brought the greatest form of ballet to America, and I was proud to be trained in his school."

"I don't know much about the ballet world," Maddie admitted, "but my mom once showed me a video of *The Nutcracker* performed by the New York City Ballet, and it was incredible. My mother likes to watch ballets when they're on television."

"I'm sure she does," Eva said, her eyes sparkling. "After all, she studied under me for years."

Maddie stared at Eva. "My mother?"

"Yes, dear. Didn't she tell you that? I assumed the reason you came to our house, when so many young people are scared away, was because she told you about me."

The young girl shook her head. "No. I never even knew my mother studied dance. I mean, I guess I knew she took lessons at some point, but had no idea it was for years."

"Are you going to tell all our secrets in one day or spread them out?" Ginny said, annoyed, from the doorway. "Lunch is ready." She turned and walked back into the kitchen.

"Ginny's right. That's enough for one day." Eva stood from her chair, and Maddie followed her to the kitchen. First, though, Maddie closed the two large doors separating off the room.

As the three sat down to eat the turkey club wraps that Ginny had made, Maddie was full of questions. "Did you build the ballet studio here? And how did you end up here, in this small town?"

"Oh, dear. Those are stories for another day," Eva said. "I hope your mother won't be upset that I told on her. I thought you'd know she was a dancer. It was something she worked at for years."

Ginny shook her head. "Always telling people things you shouldn't," she said. "Although I can't for the life of me understand why your mother would keep it a secret. She was an excellent dancer."

Maddie was surprised by Ginny's words. Ginny didn't give compliments easily.

"What about you, dear?" Eva asked. "What are your plans after you graduate high school?"

Maddie chewed her food as she thought. She wasn't accustomed to sharing anything about herself. "My parents have been asking me the same question. I'm supposed to take my ACTs in August and then begin applying to colleges. But I'm not very excited about it."

"Why? Don't you like school?" Ginny asked.

"Oh, I do well in school. I earn good grades. But I'm not

sure what I want to study in college, or where I want to go," Maddie said.

"What are your favorite classes in school?" Eva asked.

"I love English class. Especially when we're told to write stories or essays. I've kept journals for years," Maddie said.

"Ah. You want to be a writer," Eva said, her eyes sparkling. "Then you should study English and creative writing in college."

Maddie had thought about doing just that, but she also knew that making a living as a writer wasn't easy. Her mother had suggested becoming an English teacher as a day job and being a writer in her spare time, but Maddie didn't want to write as a hobby. She wanted to do it for a living.

"Hm. Suddenly so quiet," Ginny said, pushing her plate away. "What's the problem?"

Maddie sighed. "I would like to study to be a writer, but my parents think I should do something more practical, like teaching."

"Ah. I see," Eva said. "Some jobs seem like dream jobs while others are more realistic."

"Exactly," Maddie said,

"I was lucky. My mother saw my potential as a dancer right away and let me follow my dream. It was my own fault that things went badly. But she never gave up on me," Eva said. "And I'm sure your mother was pushed by her parents to find a more realistic job, so that's why she gave up dancing to attend college. Now, she doesn't realize she's doing the same to you."

"My parents are practical," Maddie said. "And they're probably right."

"Nonsense!" Ginny said, standing to put her plate in the dishwasher. "There are a lot of ways for a writer to earn a living. You could be a journalist. Or write for magazines or that infernal internet. There are many more opportunities now than in our day."

Maddie couldn't help but smile. Ginny constantly surprised her.

"Thank you for lunch," Maddie said as she brought her plate to the sink. "It was delicious. I'd better go now. I have one more lawn to mow, and then I have to work tonight at the Frosty Freeze."

Eva stood and walked Maddie to the door. "You're a hard worker, Maddie. You'll figure out how to follow your dreams. I'm sure if it."

"Thanks," Maddie said.

"The next time you mow, I'll tell you what it was like to have George Balanchine as a teacher. It was constant work—but fun as well."

"I can't wait," Maddie said. She headed down the stone steps, feeling lighthearted. She knew exactly what she was going to write about in her journal tonight after work.

* * *

After mowing the neighbor's lawn, Maddie rushed home, showered, and went downstairs to drive to the Freeze. She hoped Livie worked with her tonight so she could tell her all about Eva being a ballet dancer.

As she hurried through the kitchen to pick up her mother's car keys, Sandy entered from the living room.

"Off to work?" Sandy asked. "I hope you're going to eat before you go."

"I already ate lunch with Eva and Ginny," Maddie said. "They were nice enough to offer it to me."

"Wow. You're on a first-name basis with the ladies and eating lunch with them?" Sandy chuckled. "I remember the days when I called them Mademoiselle Arthur and Mrs. Robertson."

Maddie turned from the door. "You never told me you took dance lessons from Eva. She said you danced for years."

Sandy shrugged. "I was a kid then. It was just something I did."

"But Eva and Ginny said you were an excellent dancer. Why did you give it up?" Maddie asked.

Sandy sighed. "Because the reality of it was I needed to go to college and get an education. My parents would never have paid for me to go off to some fancy ballet school so I could eventually join a company."

"But you had a teacher trained by Balanchine. You must have been talented enough to audition for the New York City Ballet," Maddie said.

"Oh, honey," Sandy said, shaking her head. "I would have had to train at their dance school to even audition. I loved dancing, but I doubt if I was good enough to do it professionally. Mlle Arthur was a wonderful teacher, but it was just a pipe dream."

Maddie studied her mother for a moment, trying to imagine her as a ballerina. Sandy was still slender and in good shape. Maddie could almost see her as a young girl, dreaming of dancing. "I'm sorry you didn't get the chances you should have had."

Sandy looked surprised. "I think everything turned out all right."

Maddie nodded and headed out the door.

On the drive to the Freeze, all Maddie could think about was how her mother had worked all her young life at one thing, only to have to give it up and become something else. Did it bother her to have given up the dream of dancing? Or was she satisfied with her life? Up to that moment, Maddie had never even thought about her parents as children with big dreams that may not have been realized. Maybe that's why they both were encouraging her to pick a safe career instead of one that might disappoint her.

Livie wasn't working with Maddie that night, and she was stuck with grumpy Carrie. Maddie was bursting to tell someone about Eva, but she didn't want to share this story with Carrie. Instead, she worked her five-to-ten shift, then went directly home.

The house was already dark when she returned home, except for the light over the staircase. Maddie made sure the door was locked, then quietly made her way up to her room. She changed into a T-shirt and shorts, then curled up on her bed with her journal. But before writing a single word, she thought better of it. Eva's story deserved its own notebook. So, she pulled a fresh notebook out of her nightstand drawer, chose her favorite pen, and began writing what Eva had told her.

Her hand flew across the page as fast as her mind worked. There was so much she wanted to say, and she didn't want to leave out one bit of it. After a time, her hand cramped, so she stopped writing and flexed it.

As she sat there, Maddie gazed around her room. Eva had lived in a tiny apartment with her mother for years and would never have even dreamed of having her own bedroom as grand as Maddie's. When they'd arrived at Gwen's sister's apartment, they'd both been stunned at how large and beautiful it was. Maddie wondered how long Eva and her mother lived with the Crandells and what type of apartment they eventually moved to. Eva's childhood had been so different from what Maddie experienced. It made Maddie wonder how she could complain about a little thing like not having her car fixed yet when Eva didn't even have her own bedroom, let alone a car.

Maddie suddenly felt very spoiled.

The next day, Caden texted Maddie several times, but she didn't answer him. She had the day off from work and mowing and wanted to spend it with Livie. But when she texted Livie, her friend said she'd be at the gym all morning, practicing. If Maddie wanted to come and watch, it would be okay.

Maddie asked her mother if she could borrow her car to go watch Livie.

"I can drop you there," her mother said. "I have to bring Lily to gymnastics anyway."

Maddie sighed but agreed. She hated not having her own car, then remembered what she'd thought the night before. She should be thankful for what she had.

Sandy dropped the girls off, and Lily ran to the other side of the gym where her class was. Livie was practicing on the opposite side, so Maddie went to the bleachers and sat at the very top.

Livie waved and smiled, then got in line to practice her routine. She started at the corner of the mat, and after a quick run, began doing handsprings, jumps, and flips.

Maddie hadn't watched her friend in a long time and was stunned at how good she was. She knew Livie was a top-level gymnast, but she hadn't thought much about it until now.

"What did you think?" Livie asked, coming up the bleachers, breathing hard. She'd completed two more routines and was tired.

"You're amazing! Maddie said. "But since you came in

third at state, you should be, right?" She smiled. "Are you going to apply for the gymnastics program at the University of Minnesota?"

"Do I have another choice?" Livie said. "I'm going on a visit there to meet the coaches next month. They'll decide then if they think I'm good enough to join the team after senior year. If not, they might still give me another chance after we graduate."

"That's so exciting," Maddie said. "Maybe I should apply to the U of M, and we can go to the same college."

"That would be great. But if I make the team, I'll be going to class and practicing and won't have much of a college life," Livie said.

Maddie frowned. "You make it sound terrible. Don't you want to go there and be on their team?"

Livie sighed. "My parents want me to go there. Honestly, I'm not excited about the whole college thing. If it were up to me, I'd do competitions and try to work my way up to the Olympic team. But my parents said it would be better if I did that while in college."

"I get it," Maddie said. "It feels like we have to make a lot of important decisions before we are even out of high school. It's hard. I just want to enjoy my senior year, but I have the ACTs and college applications looming over my head."

"You have nothing to worry about," Livie said. "With your grades, you'll get into any college you want. Mine, on the other hand, aren't as good. But you know what?"

Maddie's brows rose in question.

"I really don't care that much about my grades," Livie continued. "I mean, I'll probably end up teaching gymnastics in a place like this for the rest of my life. Why on earth do I need a fancy diploma?"

"Maybe you can teach at a college if you have your diploma," Maddie suggested.

Livie shrugged. "Maybe. We'll see." She glanced over to where Lily's class was using the uneven parallel bars. "Lily really has what it takes to do well in gymnastics, too. I'd better get back to practice. We have a meet next week, and I want—no, I need—to win it to look good for the U of M." She hurried off toward the mats, and after stretching, started her routine again.

Maddie watched both Livie and Lily as they practiced. Livie was right. Lily was really good. Maddie had been so wrapped up in her own summer drama that she hadn't noticed how much better Lily had become.

When Sandy came to pick up Lily, Maddie went home with them, too. She went to her room and read what she'd written the night before, correcting sentences and adding more details. Maddie couldn't wait to hear more of Eva's story. She'd already decided she was going to write down everything that Eva told her, because it was such an interesting story. Maybe Ginny was right—Maddie could go to college for writing and do both journalism and creative writing. She could even attend an additional year to obtain an English teaching degree. But first, she had to get through this summer.

Chapter Seven

Eva – 1952

The first day of dance class at the School of American Ballet, (the kids called it SAB), was both exciting and scary for Eve. She was in the class of students aged eleven to thirteen, and as she watched the girls to imitate their movements, she realized they were all more advanced than she was. Even though it was intimidating, she remembered her mother's words to her when she'd left home that morning.

"Keep your eye on the best dancer in the room and aspire to be like them," Gwen had told her. "That's the way you'll learn to be the best." So, Eve did that, watching a thirteen-year-old girl and modeling herself after her.

After a few weeks of two classes a day, Eve felt like she was starting to fit in. The teachers—mostly Russian except for one English teacher and one American—were all excellent. They encouraged the girls in a positive way and corrected their stances when necessary with just a touch of the hand or a quiet suggestion. No one was made to feel less than in the group. The teachers were there to train excellent dancers and encourage them, not to tear them down mentally.

Sometimes, Mr. Balanchine, whom all the dancers called Mr. B, watched a class and whispered to the teacher. Eve never knew what they were whispering about, but when his eyes fell on her, she'd stand even straighter and work harder. She wanted to be the best dancer she could be, and something inside her wanted to make Mr. B proud and not regret giving her a chance.

As the weeks went by, Eve's life fell into a routine. She was accepted into the Professional Children's School and had morning classes there, then walked the few blocks to SAB for afternoon classes. Sometimes, she rushed to the automat two blocks away from the dance school to grab a sandwich and milk and gobble it down before dance class. Eve loved the automat. It was a place where people went to buy quick food. There were little compartments all along the wall, and she'd put her money in one, and it would open so she could buy a sandwich, a drink, a pie slice, cookies, and an array of other foods. Eve usually got a ham and cheese sandwich because she could eat it quickly.

Several of the other dancers went to the Professional Children's School, too, so Eve slowly became friends with them. They'd walk as a group from the school to dance lessons, or they'd all go to the automat together. Eve liked having the other girls with her. Even though she felt safe running around New York City on her own, it was so much more fun with friends.

One girl became her best friend. Mary Rasmussen was the blond girl who'd spoken to her after Eve's first audition. The first day of classes, Mary smiled at her and said, "I told you you'd be chosen." From that time on, they hung around together at both the school and the dance studio.

Between school and dance, Eve spent very little time at her aunt's apartment. Even though she liked living in the big, beautiful space and got along well with Ginny, she was much too busy to spend time with her cousin. And her mother had found a job at a real estate company where she worked as a typist, so Gwen and Eve only saw each other at night.

"You're so lucky you have such a short day at school," Ginny told Eve one evening while Eve worked on homework. Even though her day was short, she still had to finish a lot of the work on her own in the evenings. "I have to stay at school all day and then have piano lessons twice a week afterward."

"Well, I do get a lot of homework," Eve said, trying to make Ginny feel better. "And I have to attend at least two dance classes each day, even on Saturday."

"But you love dance, so it's not so bad," Ginny said.

"Don't you like your piano lessons?" Eve asked. She lived and breathed dancing, so to her, it would be weird not to like the lessons you chose.

Ginny shrugged. "They're okay. It's really my mother who wants me to learn piano. Did your mom push you into dance?"

"No. I love taking dance," Eve said. "I've never thought of it as work."

"Weird," Ginny said.

As the winter months flew by, Eve spent more time at the dance school. After her own classes, she'd stay later and watch the older students rehearse the different ballets created by Mr. B. Even though they hadn't yet been chosen to dance for the NYCB, they were told to learn the many parts so he could see what their strengths and weaknesses were.

Eve sat over to the side of the room, out of the way, and worked on her homework while watching them. The girls were all so accomplished and danced with ease, and they had men for partners in many of the dances. Eve was in awe of how gracefully they danced, while understanding how much work it really was to do each step perfectly.

Sometimes Mr. B would join in and show them the steps they had done incorrectly. He usually wore a plaid cowboy shirt and a string tie with trousers and his street shoes. Eve found his way of dressing amusing, since it didn't match with his Russian accent. But he always spoke quietly to the dancers, pointing out where they could jump higher or extend their arms longer.

"Jump higher!" he'd call out to a male dancer as he leapt off the floor. "Bend deeper, jump higher." Or he'd watch a girl pirouette and say, "Spin faster! What are you saving it for? Do your best now, not later."

Eve was in awe of the movements he'd get out of each dancer. Everyone wanted to please Mr. B.

Since Eve spent so much time in the studio after classes, the older girls paid her fifty cents to sew ribbons and elastic on their new pointe shoes. The older students went through several pairs of pointe shoes each month because they worked so hard in them. Eve was happy to do it. It gave her extra money to buy lunch every day, and she could splurge on a piece of pie or cake.

One evening, as she concentrated on her sewing while the music played for the dancers, a shadow appeared over her. Eve looked up, shocked to see Mr. B staring down at her.

"What is this? Child labor?" he asked with a tease in his voice.

"Oh, no, sir," Eve said, straining her neck to look up at him. "The girls pay me to sew their ribbons on."

He bent down to Eve's level. "Why are you here so late? Didn't your classes end hours ago?"

"Yes, sir," Eve said. "But I like watching the older students rehearse."

"Why?" Balanchine persisted.

"To learn," Eve said. She wondered why he didn't realize that.

Balanchine stared at her, then smiled. "Good. Good girl," he said, standing up straight again. "But make sure to charge these lazy girls a big price for your work." He smiled again and returned to the students practicing.

Eve was relieved. She'd been afraid he'd tell her she couldn't come to rehearsals and watch anymore. But he hadn't. And several times after that, Mr. B offered to walk with her on her way home. His apartment was closer to the studio than hers, but he walked her that far and then told her to run home and be safe. They rarely spoke, but she appreciated that he cared enough to make sure she got home safely.

Six months after moving to New York City, Gwen had good news for Eve.

"I've found an apartment just one block away from here for us to move into," Gwen said happily. She'd been working hard as a typist in the real estate office for months, saving her money. "It's small, but it will be ours."

Eve was excited. While she enjoyed living in Ginny's beautiful room, she preferred living alone with her mother. Neither Gwen nor Eve were home that much, so a smaller space didn't bother Eve.

The apartment was very small. It was only one room with a tiny kitchen and an even smaller bathroom. Their living room would be their bedroom. Plus, it was on the seventh floor, which meant walking up several flights of stairs each day. But it came furnished, and it was clean, so that was all that mattered.

But when Gwen's sister Bea saw the place, she was shocked. "You can't live here," she told her sister. "It's not enough room for one person, let alone two."

"We'll be fine," Gwen told her. "We've lived in worse."

Bea shook her head. "Well, those twin beds will have to go. I'll give you the trundle bed we have in storage. It'll work as a sofa during the day and two beds at night. You also need a dining room table. There's nowhere to sit! You can have our kitchen table. I've been wanting a new one anyway."

Gwen was a proud woman, but she accepted her sister's gift of furniture. Bea also had end tables and lamps brought to the apartment and paid movers to carry them all up the stairs. "There. Now at least it's livable."

Eve was happy to have the table, even if they rarely ate dinner there. It was a space where she could do homework at night. If they ate dinner at all, Gwen usually brought home something from the cafeteria down the street. If Eve stayed late at the studio, she always ate at the automat.

All through the winter, Eve never missed school or dance classes. Even when it was so cold, her fingers and toes froze on her walk to school. Occasionally, Mr. B came to watch the class, and if he noticed students were missing, he'd frown. She knew he expected students not to miss class unless it was an emergency. Eve didn't want to do anything that would cause her scholarship to be taken away.

She lived and breathed dancing. Eve never thought of it as work, even when it was difficult. It's all she'd ever wanted to do, and if it meant hard work to succeed, she was willing to do that.

That spring, she learned that they had summers off. Eve was progressing so well, she hated taking that much time off from classes. When she asked the administrator if she could attend the summer session, the woman told her that was decided by Mr. Balanchine. So, she placed her name on the list and crossed her fingers that she'd be chosen.

"Dear, you could always take lessons with another dance teacher during the summer," Gwen told Eve.

"But it's important that I keep learning the technique they teach at SAB. Mr. B wants students taught his way," Eve said.

"Well, let's hope they choose you then," Gwen said. What she didn't tell Eve was that she might not be able to afford the lessons at SAB for the summer, especially if Eve didn't get another scholarship for the next year.

Luckily for Eve, Mr. B saw her name on the list and approved her attendance at the summer session. When Eve saw him one evening in the hallway, she thanked him profusely for letting her attend the summer classes.

"Dear," he said softly. "You deserved it. I know you work hard. Tell your mother all is taken care of and that you will have a scholarship for next year as well."

Eve's mouth dropped open. Even at her young age, she knew how important it was for them to receive help for her dance lessons. "Oh, thank you, Mr. B," she said excitedly.

He smiled. "Make me proud." Then he sauntered off down the hallway.

Gwen was thrilled to hear that SAB had offered to pay for Eve's lessons all summer and for the next year. She wrote a thank-you letter to Mr. Balanchine and the school. He never responded, but it didn't matter. All that mattered was for Eve to continue dancing.

Near the end of the regular school year, Eve was watching the older students practice dances they'd use for auditions in case they weren't invited to dance for NYCB. She was sewing ribbons on one of the girls' shoes as she watched. Mr. B was also in the room, watching the dancers, but suddenly stood and shook his head.

"No, no, no, dear," he told the young dancer. "You are supposed to end with a demi-pointe attitude arabesque. Try again."

The girl began again. She started in second position, pointing her foot in the direction she was moving. Then she did a glissade, a pirouette en pointe, and ended in the demi-pointe attitude arabesque. But each time, she faltered and ended up flat-footed in the arabesque.

"It's a difficult step," she said after trying twice.

"Bah! A child could do that step," Mr. B said. His head turned to Eve.

Eve looked up and saw all the students staring at her. She didn't understand why.

"Dear. Come over here a moment, please, and show these dancers how to do this step," Mr. B said, looking at Eve.

Eve's eyes scanned the room as her heart beat faster. She'd been watching, so she knew the steps, but to show these older, advanced students how to do a dance was insane.

"Come along. I know you can do this," Mr. B said, his eyes watching hers.

Eve was still wearing her dance clothes with a sweater over them. She stood, slipped off her oversized sweater, and walked over to the front of the group.

"Have you been watching?" Mr. B asked. "Do you know the steps?"

Eve nodded. She swallowed hard, then took the beginning position. The piano began to play, and on the second count,

Eve moved her feet—*glissade, pirouette, demi-pointe, attitude arabesque.* Eve stood in arabesque for a moment, then lowered her leg.

"Do attitude arabesque again," Mr. B said.

Eve did, and Mr. B walked up to her, placing his arms wide. "See this? This is the perfect stance, leg bent just so, shoulder's back, straight leg on demi-pointe. Now, do you think it is so hard?" he asked the older dancer.

He turned to Eve. "Thank you, Eva." He'd pronounced her name as *Ava.*

She dropped her leg and walked back to the sidelines. Eve hoped the other students wouldn't hate her for being able to perform a step they couldn't.

After she had finished sewing the ribbons on the dancer's pointe shoes, she set them near the girl's bag and quietly headed for the door. The class had finished by then, and the dancers were stretching. Mr. B had left already.

"Good job, Eva," the older student said, running up to her, smiling. "You're quite advanced for your age. Keep it up."

The other students all nodded and waved at her. Eve sighed. She was glad they weren't angry with her.

"Oh, Eva," a dancer came over and handed her fifty cents. "Thanks for sewing my shoes. I'll miss having your help if I'm chosen by a dance company. Good luck next year." She ran back to the barre where her bag and shoes were.

As Eve walked home, she thought about Mr. B and the dancers calling her Eva instead of Eve. Her mother had said she should change her name when she became a dancer. Maybe her mother was right. She could be Evalina, with Eva for short. She had liked how it sounded when Mr. B had said it in his Russian accent.

"Evalina Ashford," Eve said aloud. "Maybe someday, I'll be famous."

She could only hope.

CHAPTER EIGHT

Maddie

Maddie sat listening to Eva's story, absorbing it all. She could picture Eva as a young girl with long, graceful limbs, her red hair pulled up in the Balanchine Bun, as she called it, and her blue eyes bright and sparkling. Even now, at her advanced age, Eva still had twinkling eyes and that impish smile that made you like her immediately.

"Your childhood must have been incredible," Maddie said. "Going to school with other child dancers and actors, taking dance classes from famous ballerinas, and knowing Balanchine. Did you feel like it was special at the time?"

"I felt grateful for the chance to learn to dance from the great teachers," Eva said. "It sounds like a fun life, but it was work. And my mother and I didn't have a normal life."

"I've told you a million times that a 'normal' life wasn't as interesting as your life was," Ginny said. She had made them all grilled cheese sandwiches and set out the usual array of raw vegetables with ranch dip. "I had a normal life. Long school hours, piano lessons, dinner at six with the family, homework, and practically no freedom. You were running all over New York City alone at all hours of the day and night and eating at the automat. I envied you back then."

"But you had a stable life," Eva said. "I was always on the go. But the dance school expected us all to behave and not get into trouble outside the school, so I was always good. And in those days, it was safe to run around the city. I'd never let a child do such a thing anymore."

"Well, I am grateful that I had a bedroom of my own and lived in a nice apartment with my family," Ginny said. "Your one-room apartment wasn't glamorous at all. But I give credit to your mother for working so hard to give you a chance at your dream."

Eva nodded. "Yes. She did work hard. And she always encouraged me. Without her, I don't know what I would have done after, well, after what happened."

Maddie's eyebrows rose. "After what happened?"

"Enough stories for today," Ginny said, getting up to clear the dishes.

"Oh, sure," Maddie said. She also stood and brought her plate to the sink. "The grilled cheese was delicious. You must have used several different cheeses, because it was so good."

"I did, but I won't give you my secret," Ginny said with a twinkle in her eye.

"Will you write down what I've told you?" Eva asked, still sitting at the table. She suddenly looked tired.

"Yes," Maddie said. "As soon as I'm finished working today. You had an amazing life."

"You're writing all this down?" Ginny asked, looking surprised. "Well, make sure to describe me as young, beautiful, and sweet." She grinned.

Maddie laughed. "Absolutely."

Maddie left after that and mowed another neighbor's yard. Once she arrived home, she showered, dressed, and sat on her bed with her notebook, writing down everything Eva had said.

"What are you up to?" Sandy asked, bringing in a pile of folded clothes for Maddie to hang.

"Eva has been telling me about her childhood studying at The School of American Ballet," Maddie said, setting her pen on her notepad. "It's so interesting that I've been writing it down."

"Oh." Sandy looked surprised. She sat on the end of Maddie's bed. "Mlle Arthur never spoke about her time at the school or dancing with the New York City Ballet when I was studying with her. We all just assumed she'd grown older and couldn't dance anymore. Although I knew she had connections at NYCB."

"She couldn't have been too old when you took lessons," Maddie said. "Weren't you a child in the late '80s and early '90s?"

Sandy chuckled. "I suppose she was my age now back then, but as children, you think someone in their forties is old. But when you think about it, dancing professionally in ballet after age thirty-five was rare in her day."

"I suppose that's true," Maddie said. "She hasn't told me yet why she stopped dancing for the NYCB."

Sandy stood. "Well, I certainly don't know. She was a very secretive person years ago. Then again, she was my teacher, and I was young, so she wouldn't have confided in me."

Maddie frowned.

"What?" Sandy asked.

"I wonder why she's confiding in me. She barely knows me."

Sandy smiled. "She must have sensed you would listen.

Maybe she thought it was time to tell her story."

Maddie nodded. Whatever the reason, she was happy Eva was sharing her story with her. "Hey, Mom?"

Sandy was at the door. She turned. "Yes."

"Do you miss dancing? I mean, to take lessons for twelve years and then give it up, you must think about it sometimes," Maddie said.

Sandy suddenly looked sad. "I do miss it sometimes. Mlle Arthur asked me several times if I'd like to teach with her during my summer breaks from college. But I declined. It actually would have been a good summer job. I guess I was afraid I'd miss dancing more if I started teaching it."

Maddie thought this over. "Is that why you had me take ballet with the other teacher in town?"

"Oh, no," Sandy said. "By then, Mlle Arthur had closed the school. I would have definitely taken you there if it were open."

"I guess I wasn't dancing material," Maddie said, smiling. "I quit after two years."

"You were only six when you started. You wouldn't have even known if you liked it or not," Sandy said. "I had you try it to see if it interested you."

"You should go and visit Eva and Ginny sometime," Maddie said. "They'd love to see you."

Sandy nodded. "You're right. I'll try to stop over there sometime."

After her mother left, Maddie continued writing Eva's story. She quit long enough to have dinner with the family, then went right back to it. By nine o'clock, she'd finished, and her phone buzzed with a text message.

"Hey, Mads. You want to sneak out of the house and hang out?" Caden texted.

Maddie sighed. That was the last thing she needed. To get caught sneaking out. *"No, I can't,"* she texted back.

"Aw, come on, Mads. Let's go have some fun. We don't do anything together anymore," Caden replied.

"I can't risk it. You know why," Maddie texted. She waited for a reply, but then the phone went quiet, so she set it down and got ready for bed. When she picked up her phone later, there was another message from Caden.

"What about going out on the boat with Aaron and me tomorrow? You could bring Livie, too. Aaron has a thing for her."

Maddie thought about it for a moment. She hadn't had much fun this summer and had a whole summer of work ahead of her. Plus, she didn't have to mow any yards or work at the Freeze tomorrow. She wasn't sure about Livie, though. She was always busy, too.

"Please!" Caden texted.

"Well, he did say please," Maddie said aloud to herself. *"OK,"* she texted. *"It sounds like fun."*

"Great!" Caden answered. *"It'll be fun! See you at Aaron's house at ten."*

Maddie texted Livie to see if she wanted to go, too. She did, so they made a plan for Livie to come to Maddie's house, and they'd drive together to Aaron's.

Aaron's parents had a beautiful house on Cedar Lake, and they had their choice of a pontoon or speedboat to take out for the day. Of course, Aaron chose the speed boat so they could waterski. But first, Aaron drove out to the middle of the lake, and they lay around in the sun in their swimsuits. Aaron passed around water and soda, then grinned mischievously at Caden.

"I've got some beer for anyone who wants to have a really good time," Aaron said.

Caden reached for one, but both Livie and Maddie declined.

"You'll lose your parents' boat if you're caught with alcohol," Maddie said, staring hard at Aaron.

He shrugged. "No one is going to check us. They never do." He swigged down half of his beer.

Maddie and Livie sat in the back of the boat on the soft cushions, and she excitedly told Livie all about Eva's life.

"Wow. That's cool that she danced for Balanchine," Livie said. "I don't know much about ballet, except for that couple of years you and I took classes, but I know who George Balanchine is."

"What's a Balanchine?" Caden asked, dropping down on the seat next to Maddie.

"Don't be rude. He's considered one of the greatest dance choreographers of all time," Maddie said. "I've been reading about him since Eva mentioned him. He lived in the Soviet Union during the revolution and WWI when Tsar Nicholas II abdicated, and then his family was killed. Years later, Balanchine was with a dance troupe in Europe and was basically smuggled into the United States with questionable paperwork. But this rich guy, Lincoln Kirstein, was determined to bring Balanchine to America to start a ballet theater and dance company."

"That's cool," Livie said. She brushed her short, brown hair out of her face with her fingers. "Gymnastics has a lot of moves like ballet. Taking those ballet classes when I was younger helped me with my training when I started gymnastics."

"This is all boring," Caden said, getting up and tossing his beer can in the small garbage bag. "Let's waterski!"

They spent the afternoon alternating between waterskiing and lazing around in the sun. Caden was good at waterskiing, but Maddie wasn't, so she declined. Caden, Livie, and Aaron skied while taking turns driving the boat.

They all had a fun time and even parked the boat at the dock in town for a few minutes to grab lunch at the Frosty Freeze. By late afternoon, they were all tired and overbaked from the sun, so they decided to go back to Aaron's house.

"Make sure those beer cans are tied up in that bag and hidden," Aaron said to Caden. "I can't risk my parents finding them."

"Ah. Your dad will think they're his," Caden said. "I've seen how he pounds them back."

Aaron glared at Caden. "Hey! Just get rid of them."

"Fine, fine." He turned to Maddie. "Want me to drive you home?"

Maddie studied Caden. She wasn't sure how many beers he'd had, but his pupils were dilated, and he was unsteady on his feet. "No. I'll ride with Livie," she said. "But maybe you should let us take you home. You shouldn't be driving."

"Oh, don't be such babies," Caden said. "I'm fine."

Maddie was worried. Caden was definitely drunk. "Why don't you stay at Aaron's for a while? That would be okay, wouldn't it, Aaron?"

Aaron nodded. "Yeah. You shouldn't be driving, Caden. Stay, and we'll have some snacks. My parents won't be home until tonight."

Caden's face scrunched up in anger. "Stop telling me what to do," he told Aaron, then he turned on Maddie. "You, too. Why do you care anyway? You never want to see me, and now you want to boss me around?"

Maddie wasn't sure what to do. She glanced over at Aaron, who shrugged.

"Hey! Why are you looking at him?" Caden asked angrily.

"Just stay here," Aaron told Caden. "Maddie and Livie could stay, too, and we'll order a pizza."

"Yeah. That's a great idea," Livie said. She grabbed her bag and towel out of the boat and headed up the lawn toward the house with Aaron.

"Come on, Cade," Maddie said, getting her bag. "I'll stay if you will."

Caden narrowed his eyes like he was going to fight about it, but then gave in. "Yeah. Pizza sounds good."

Maddie was relieved. She put her arm through Caden's and walked beside him up to the house.

Later, when Livie drove Maddie home, she expressed her concern about Caden.

"Caden has been a little off the rails lately, don't you think?" Livie asked. "I mean, today was a bit tense."

Maddie nodded. "I don't know what's going on with him. I mean, I know I've been mad at him for ruining my car and then not offering to pay, but I haven't broken up with him. He acts like everything should be just fine. Meanwhile, I have to work all the time to pay for my car repairs."

"That isn't fair," Livie said. "But Caden is kind of irresponsible."

"He is." Maddie turned to Livie. "Has he always been like that, and I just didn't see it? Or have my priorities changed?"

"Well," Livie said. "Don't get mad at me, but he's always acted like this. Remember all the times last year he tried to talk you into going to drinking parties in the woods? You even went with him once and said you hated it. It's like he doesn't care if he does well in school or gets caught doing something stupid."

Maddie mused this over for a while. That one time last

summer that she agreed to go to the bonfire party had been a disaster. Caden kept chugging beer from the keg and then threw up in his truck. Maddie had to drive him home, then called her mother to pick her up. Luckily, she hadn't drunk anything and didn't smell like beer.

"I had hoped he'd grown up a little this year," Maddie finally said. "I really care about him, but he seems to be getting worse. I don't know what to do."

They had pulled into Maddie's driveway, and Livie put her car in park. "I don't know what to tell you, Mads. Just make sure you don't let Caden take you down with him. You're smart and definitely need to go to college, and you don't want him to ruin that for you."

"I know. It's just hard." Maddie said goodbye and went inside the house. Her mother was sitting on the sofa, watching a late-night program. Maddie figured Lily and her father had already gone to bed.

"Are you waiting up for me?" Maddie asked, dropping onto the sofa. "I texted earlier to let you know we were eating dinner at Aaron's house."

"I know," Sandy said. "And I appreciated that. I guess after the accident last spring, I still worry about you being out late with Caden."

Maddie sighed. "I don't let him drive me home anymore. Either I drive, or Livie does."

Sandy nodded. "I'm glad you do that. I just worry, that's all."

Maddie wanted to be mad at her mother for not trusting her, but she also understood. "You don't like Caden either, do you? Like Dad doesn't like him."

"Oh, honey," Sandy said, turning the television down. "It

doesn't matter what your father or I think of Caden. We want what's best for you. And we want you to choose what's best for you, not us."

"I know," Maddie said.

Sandy leaned closer to her. "Honey, you have your whole life ahead of you. Senior year can be so much fun, and then college. I don't want anything stupid, like a car accident, to ruin your future. And I'm afraid that Caden isn't on the same path as you. He's, well, he seems to be more about having fun and less about thinking about his future. Is he even planning to go to college or some kind of extended learning after high school?"

"He hasn't said what he wants to do," Maddie said. "But I'm not sure yet where I want to go either. I won't know until after the ACTs."

"Is Caden taking the ACTs in August?" Sandy asked.

Maddie shrugged. "I haven't asked him. We aren't getting along well right now, and today we all had fun for a change."

Sandy patted Maddie's arm. "Well, I hope he decides to do something with his future. I'd like to see Caden succeed, just like I want you and Lily to. Life gets harder as you get older, so do everything you can to make sure you have a good life. College is part of that."

"I know," Maddie said. "I'll definitely go to college." She stood. "I'm tired. Tomorrow, I have two lawns to mow and then a shift at the Freeze."

Sandy smiled. "I hope you know how proud I am of you, dear. You're working hard to pay us back, and we appreciate it."

"Thanks, Mom. I know I screwed up letting Caden drive my car. It won't happen again."

Sandy nodded. "I know. You're too smart to let it." She

turned up the television and sat back on the sofa.

Maddie went upstairs and showered off the sand from that day. When she crawled into bed, she pulled out her notebook with Eva's story written in it. She began reading what she'd written from the beginning and started correcting and changing words to make it read better. She was looking forward to next week when she visited with Eva and Ginny again. Maddie couldn't wait to hear more about her life with the ballet.

CHAPTER NINE

Eva – 1954

Eve was so excited. In September, she'd been told by the ballet mistress that she'd been chosen along with several other young dancers to be one of the children in the party scene of *The Nutcracker*. Mr. B invited students from SAB whenever he had roles for younger dancers. So, in addition to taking two classes a day after going to school, Eve also started rehearsals for her small part in the seasonal ballet.

The ballet had premiered that same year in February and returned for the holiday season. There would be performances twice daily from the end of November until the first of January. Because of the many performances, Eve was a part of one of two groups of children who would participate.

They practiced in one of SAB's larger studios. What looked like an easy part when watching the ballet, of children running around and having fun, was actually quite complicated. They each had their places to be and must run from spot to spot in unison. With so many children running about, it was confusing. Eve listened intently to the teachers while they each learned their part and was even more attentive when Mr. B dropped by to see how the children were coming along.

"Above all else," Mr. B said with his thick accent. "This is supposed to be fun. So, learn your parts well, but have fun with it. It's not the end of the world if you miss your spot or end at the wrong place. Just fix your mistake quietly and continue. So much is going on in the ballet that no one is going to notice an errant mistake or two."

Eve's mother was beyond excited about her daughter's chance to appear in a ballet. "I'm telling everyone I work with to go see the performance," Gwen said. "At only twelve, my daughter is already dancing on stage."

"But, Mom," Eve protested. "I'll only be in half of the performances. The other group is doing the other half. How will your friends know which time to buy tickets for?"

Gwen waved her hand through the air. "They won't know the difference. I'll tell them what dress you'll be wearing, and they'll look for you. Even if it's not you, my friends won't know."

Eve thought that was funny. But it was also true. There were so many dancers in *The Nutcracker* that it would be hard to pick out one person unless they were dancing a solo.

All the children were fitted for costumes, and by the time they had a dress rehearsal at the State Theater, each child had a costume tagged with their name. Since *The Nutcracker* was set in the 1800s, all the younger girls wore ankle-length, frilly dresses and long pantaloons along with their ballet slippers. They were told to arrive at the theater two hours before the performance and have their hair styled beforehand. The costume designer suggested ways to do their hair that would look appropriate with the old-fashioned costumes.

Eve's friend, Mary, was also cast as one of the girls and was excited to be dancing in the same group. Eve had long, thick auburn hair that her mother could easily style, and Mary's long, blond hair could be styled nicely, too. They giggled with excitement after each rehearsal, but the day of the dress rehearsal, with Mr. B overseeing it, the girls were nervous. This was it. They were actually going to perform on stage.

When all the children ran into the room with the beautiful tree and gifts everywhere, Eve paid attention to where she was supposed to stand and where to move. It looked so different with the backgrounds set up and the many dancers on the stage than in rehearsals. It was downright confusing. But she tried her best to stay with the group of girls and not make a mistake.

"Smiles, children," Mr. B called out. "It's Christmas, not a funeral. You should be happy and joyous."

His comments made the children smile, and after a bit, Eve relaxed and moved with the flow of the children, as she'd been taught.

"Have fun!" Mr. B called out. "Be cheerful! You are here to make others happy."

By the end of her part of the rehearsal, Eve was tired but had calmed down immensely. Mr. B's mood had been cheerful and encouraging throughout the rehearsal, and it had helped her feel confident she could remember her part.

After changing, she went into the auditorium to watch the grown-up dancers rehearse. The entire ballet was complicated and beautiful. From the snowflake dancers to the Sugar-Plum Fairy, their dancing was amazing. Eve knew that one of the principal dancers was Mr. B's new wife, known as Tanny to all. Another was Maria Tallchief, his ex-wife. It seemed confusing to a young person like Eve, but both women danced beautifully, and she understood that was the most important thing to Mr. B.

As the day drew near for the actual performance, Betty Cage, the NYCB's company manager—who Eve thought did everything—asked all the young dancers what name they'd like her to put on the program for the ballet.

"Evalina Ashford," Eve said proudly.

Betty's brows shot up, then she smiled. "That's a wonderful name for a prima ballerina," she said with a wink.

That evening, when Eve went home, she told her mother what name she'd had them place on the programs.

"I love it! See, I make good suggestions sometimes," Gwen said, laughing. "Always think big. That will make your dreams come true."

After that day, everyone called her Eva instead of Eve, except for family members who'd forget about the name change. Since Mr. B had already christened her Eva, most of the dancers already called her that name.

The first performance of *The Nutcracker* was an evening performance the weekend after Thanksgiving. Eva's group was chosen to perform that night. Nervous, Eva appeared at the theater with her mother, her hair already half up, half down with a long ribbon tied in it. Gwen left her backstage to go to her seat, which Mr. B had graciously given her a ticket for.

Eva weaved her way through the many dancers to the small room where all the little girls would change into their costumes. More than one hundred and fifty dancers performed in the ballet, making the backstage area a busy, confusing place.

Eva found the small room, not much bigger than a closet, where the other girls were. They were giggling and helping each other zip or button their dresses. Mary was there, which made Eva less nervous. The girls wore tights underneath their long pantaloons and the full-skirted dresses. In the stuffy little room, they all grew hot quickly, so they opened the door for some air and stood in the doorway, watching the craziness of performers, stagehands, and other workers.

"We should stretch, shouldn't we?" Eva asked the group. She had seen the older dancers at the barres around the backstage area warming up.

The girls stood in a circle in the room and did several pliés and lunges, stretching their muscles for all the running around they'd be doing on stage. Soon, one of their teachers came to the room.

"Follow me to your places," she said. They all followed her in a nice little line like perfect little ballerinas. The older dancers turned and smiled at them.

"Take your places, ladies," the ballet teacher said quietly. "You and the boys will all go in with the adults after the portion with Clara."

Eva waited anxiously with the crowd around her. There were the young girls, the young boys, and several adults playing the parents. The music from the orchestra swelled, and the ballet began. Eva took a deep breath. Suddenly, she and the entire group were swept onto the stage, onto a set that looked like a grand living room with a beautiful Christmas tree. The ballet had begun.

Once on stage, Eva's training kicked in, and she was no longer nervous. She only thought of where she belonged in the group and followed along perfectly. So much was happening. Kids were running around, playing different games. The girls sat in a circle for a moment, then, after receiving their presents—dolls—they sat together to play with Clara. Dancers playing parents chattered and moved around them.

At one point, Eva noticed that the long dresses were

hampering their movements, and more than one girl would stand quickly, only to step on her dress and hit the floor again. After noticing this, Eva was careful to always make sure her dress pooled around her when she sat on the floor so she wouldn't trip. At another part of the ballet, Eva saw Mary moving in the wrong direction, and she quickly took her hand and guided her back. Eva was so involved in the scene happening around her, she knew by heart exactly what she was supposed to do.

Much to her surprise, she remembered the music, and it guided her through the first act. She was attuned to it on stage, more than she'd been in rehearsal. She not only heard it, she felt it just as Mr. B had always said. "Feel the music, dear. There is no dance without music."

After the children's scene was finished, the group ran off stage to change, right past Mr. B standing in the wings. He reached out his hand and patted the children on the head as they passed. "Good work. Good work," he said, smiling. When Eva passed him, he smiled and winked. That was all she needed from him, because it meant he'd seen her out there and approved.

After changing out of her costume and carefully hanging it up, Eva snuck back to the wings and made herself small. She wanted to watch the dancers from here. It was such a different perspective, watching from the wings as the dancers rushed on and off stage. Even though Eva knew this was all make-believe with elaborate sets and costumes, she understood how much work each dancer had put into this ballet. To her, it was all magical. And she knew then and there that she wanted to be a part of that magic, forever.

* * *

Eva's Aunt Bea brought Ginny to one of the matinee performances Eva was in, and Ginny marveled afterward at how amazing her cousin was.

"I can't believe you were on stage with all those dancers!" Ginny said, sounding in awe of her. "Were you scared?"

"I was the first night," Eva admitted. "But once I was on stage, it was like my body took over and I did everything the way I'd learned it. Mr. B says not to think, just do. He's right. If you don't overthink it, your training kicks in."

"Oh, I could never do that," Ginny said. "To be on stage in front of all those people. I'd die!"

Eva swelled with pride. It took a lot to impress the city-born Ginny. "Well, that's what I'm training to do. If I were scared to go on stage, that would be awful."

Eva and her mother celebrated Christmas with Bea and her family that year, but also put up a small tree in their own apartment. Life was going well for them. Gwen had been promoted from typist to assistant secretary for one of the real estate agents and had also received a raise. She was also dating an agent from her office, which made her very happy. Even though Eva hadn't yet met the man, she was happy for her mother.

By spring, however, everything fell apart. Gwen learned the man she'd been dating was married, and she broke it off with him. All Eva knew was that she had broken up with the man, but not why. And then, out of the blue, Gwen was fired from her job. The man had spoken badly about her to Gwen's boss, and he reluctantly let her go.

"What are we going to do?" Eva asked. "Will we have to leave our apartment?"

"I hope not, honey," Gwen said one evening when they both were home together. "I'll hit the pavement every day until

I find something."

"What about my schooling? And dancing?" Eva asked in a small voice. "I've already asked to be a part of the summer session again this year."

Gwen sighed. "Let's hope Mr. Balanchine will be generous again this year and offer you a scholarship for summer classes. But I promise, dear. Even if we have to pay, I'll do whatever it takes to keep you in the dance school."

Eva worried every day that her mother couldn't find a job. Bea told them they could move in with them again, but Gwen resisted. She was determined to find a job.

Eva continued to stay late to watch rehearsals at SAB and offered to sew pointe shoes for the girls. She made enough money each day to buy her own lunch so her mother wouldn't have to worry about it. Eva was now thirteen, and next fall she'd be in classes with the older students. She couldn't wait.

Mr. B continued to notice her staying late. He'd smile at her or say hello as he watched rehearsals. One evening, he walked over to her as she sewed ribbons on pointe shoes.

"How old are you now, Eva?" he asked, studying her.

"Thirteen." Eva looked up at him.

He tilted his head. "You should be sewing ribbons on your own toe shoes," he said. "You have strong arches, and I think you are now ready for them. Tell the ballet mistress tomorrow to have you fitted for shoes, and once you get them, you may start taking pointe classes in addition to your other daily classes."

Eva's heart pounded with joy. She'd dreamed of the time when she could start pointe classes. That was one step closer to becoming a true ballerina. "Yes, sir. Thank you." She sprang from her seat on the floor and hugged him.

Mr. B smiled. "You are so welcome, dear. I expect to see you here in rehearsals someday, dancing these very steps."

"I can't wait," she told him.

That night, she rushed home and told her mother she was going to get pointe shoes. Gwen was excited for her but also knew that the shoes were an extra expense.

"Oh." Eva's excitement faded. "I thought they were part of the tuition. I can save my money and help buy them," she told her mother.

Gwen smiled at her. "Dear. We'll make it happen. Don't you worry."

When Eva went to the ballet mistress the next day to tell her Mr. B had said she should be fitted for pointe shoes, the woman nodded.

"Yes, dear. He left me a note," The woman said. She took measurements and wrote them down. "For now, we just get the right size," the woman said. "When you start dancing, we'll have them specially designed for your feet. But that is a few years away."

Eva nodded, not quite understanding but pretending to.

"The shoes are eight dollars and fifty cents a pair," the ballet mistress said.

Eva's heart sank. It might as well have been eight hundred and fifty dollars.

"Don't worry, dear," the woman said, seeing her distressed expression. "Your scholarship will pay for them. Take good care of your shoes, and they should work well for you until you grow out of them."

"Oh, thank you, Madame," Eva said. "I'll take good care of them."

"And once you get them, have one of the older girls teach

you how to break them in before you start class. Otherwise, it's like dancing in wooden shoes."

"Yes, Madame," Eva said. She'd watched the older girls hitting their new pointe shoes on the floor, bending them, sitting on them, and doing all sorts of things to soften them up. She'd ask one of the girls at rehearsals to tell her what to do.

A week later, after sewing on the elastic and ribbons and learning how to break down the shoes so they'd bend, Eva took her first pointe class. It was between her other two classes, with other thirteen- and fourteen-year-old students. Eva had softened her shoes a little, but not enough to break them, so they'd last longer. As she stood at the barre, practicing the many familiar steps she did in regular class, it felt like she was relearning everything she'd already mastered. The relevés in all positions were harder, and demi-pointe was difficult. But she kept up as best as she could with the other students.

After class, the teacher told her she'd done well for a first timer. "Keep it up," the elderly woman said. "You have good balance and strong arches. You will do well."

Eva swelled up with pride. She would work hard and do her best.

When she arrived home that evening, her mother was there already and had bought a small cake from the bakery.

"What's this?" Eva asked. She knew they had little extra money to spend.

"Congratulations on your first day of pointe class!" Gwen told her. "And congrats to me, too. I found a new job today!"

"Oh, mom!" Eva hugged her mother. "I'm so happy. Where is it?"

Gwen beamed. "I'll be working for a smaller real estate office, but as the main secretary for both men who work there.

And the pay is higher than at my last job."

"That's wonderful," Eva squealed. "We both had exciting days today."

Gwen got a knife and two plates and cut each of them a piece of cake. It was chocolate with whipped white frosting. Eva thought it was delicious.

"I really have a good feeling about this job," Gwen told Eva. "I think we are both on our way up."

Eva was both excited and relieved. Now, she wouldn't have to worry about having to quit ballet school if she didn't get a scholarship next year. After today, she knew she only wanted to dance at that school and for that ballet company. She wanted to dance for Mr. B.

Chapter Ten

Maddie

"It must be hard to dance in pointe shoes," Maddie said after Eva had paused telling her story. "How long was it before you were used to them?"

Eva laughed. "Years! But I loved dancing on pointe. It was a whole new experience. All the practice a dancer does up to that point prepares them to dance in pointe shoes. Once you get your bearings, it's like dancing on air."

"I would have loved to have seen you dance," Maddie said, enthralled. "I don't suppose there are any videos online of you dancing."

Eva shrugged. "Possibly, but I've never seen any. There is some old film of Suzanne Farrell, one of my contemporaries, but most are grainy. I was two years older than Suzanne when she joined the company, but she surpassed us all. She became Mr. B's favorite dancer throughout the 1960s, and for good reason. She was an incredible dancer and had a close relationship with him."

Maddie had never heard of Suzanne Farrell before, so she

made a mental note to look her up. She wanted to know everything to do with Eva's story.

Ginny served lunch—this time she made homemade chicken noodle soup with crackers—and Maddie continued questioning Eva. But by the end of lunch, Maddie saw that Eva was getting tired, so she made an excuse to leave.

"Thank you for lunch," Maddie said to Ginny. "It was delicious."

"Sure, sure," Ginny said in her offhanded way.

"You'll come by next week again, won't you?" Eva asked. She'd moved to the small living room and sat down on the sofa.

"Yes. Definitely," Maddie said with a smile. "Would it be okay for my mom to come, too? I know she'd like to see you both."

"Oh, that would be wonderful," Eva said, her face brightening.

Maddie left after that and rode the lawnmower home. Her mother and sister had already left for Lily's gymnastic class. Maddie showered and sat on her bed to write more of Eva's story in her notebook. She was fascinated by Eva's dedication to dancing at such a young age. Except for her friend Livie, Maddie hadn't known many young people who lived and breathed their sport or other activities. Although Maddie had always loved writing and wrote often, it was nothing like Eva's training.

Maddie's mom hadn't returned with the car by the time Maddie had to work at the Freeze, so she called Livie to ask if she was working that night. When Livie didn't answer, she had no other option but to call Caden for a ride.

"Yeah. Sure. Call me when you need something," Caden said after she asked him to drive her to work.

"Fine. I'll walk if I have to," Maddie told him, annoyed by his attitude.

"I was just giving you a hard time," Caden said. "I'll come get you."

He didn't honk this time when he pulled into the driveway, but neither of Maddie's parents was home, so it didn't matter. She slid into his truck.

"Thanks. I wouldn't have bothered you if I hadn't needed a ride," Maddie said.

Caden sighed.

"What?"

"I just wish we were going out tonight instead of you going to work," Caden said. "I miss the old days. We had so much fun together."

"I miss them, too," Maddie admitted. "But I'm so busy. This is what real life is like, you know. My parents work all the time and never have time for fun. When we graduate high school, we'll be like that, too."

"Not me," Caden insisted. "I plan to enjoy my life, not work it away."

Maddie watched him as he drove. "Are you taking the ACTs in August? Both Livie and I are scheduled to take them."

Caden laughed. "With my grades? It would be a waste of time and money."

Maddie was disappointed. "There's a refresher course just for the ACTs the week before the test. I'll be doing that, too. You could still sign up."

He shook his head. "I'm not college material, Mads. You know that."

"What about tech school?" she asked.

"Nope. Not gonna go."

"What are your plans after high school?" Maddie asked. Everyone she knew had a plan, even if it was to get a job somewhere.

"I have a job at the car wash. Or I can find something at an oil change place," Caden said. "Something will come up."

Maddie wasn't opposed to him only working after high school, but it bothered her that he didn't have any plans for his future.

Caden pulled up to the side door of the Freeze. "Hey. Why don't you let me pick you up tonight after work?" he asked. "There's a party out at a friend's cabin. It'll be fun."

"I can't," Maddie said. "If I were caught at an underage drinking party, I'd lose my car forever."

"You're such a goody-two-shoes," Caden said snidely. "Our teenage years are supposed to be fun."

"They can be fun without breaking laws," Maddie shot back. She stepped out of his truck. "Thanks for the ride." She was about to shut the door, then turned back. "Caden?"

"Yeah."

"Be careful, okay?" Maddie meant it. No matter what was going on between them, she didn't want to see him hurt.

"Yeah, yeah," he said offhandedly. As soon as Maddie shut the door, he sped off.

Annoyed, Maddie walked into the building, hoping she didn't have to work with Carrie tonight. The last thing she needed was someone else in a bad mood. So, she was happy to see Livie at the till.

"Are you working tonight?" Maddie asked.

"Yeah. Sorry, I missed your call," Livie said. "My mom was lecturing me on how I need to get my head into my gymnastics, or else I won't be offered a scholarship. No scholarship, no college."

Maddie frowned. "That's a lot of pressure."

Livie nodded. "But it's a lot of pressure on my parents, too. I know they want me to go to college, but they could never afford it, and our family income doesn't qualify us for grants or low-interest loans. It frustrates my mom that we're at that middle income that is too much but not enough."

"That is frustrating," Maddie said. "Hopefully you'll be offered a spot on the team at U of M."

"Yeah. Hopefully." Livie sighed.

Maddie went into the back room to lock up her small bag and put on her apron. Between the way Caden was acting and what was happening in her own life and Livie's, everyone was stressed.

Halfway through her shift, Sandy texted Maddie to ask how she got to work.

"Caden drove me," Maddie texted back. *"Livie can drive me home."*

"Okay, good," Sandy texted. *"Sorry, we weren't back in time to let you use the car. Lily stayed late to talk to her coach about the next meet."*

"That's OK," Maddie texted. Even her little sister was under pressure to perform.

The night went by quickly as they served up burgers, chicken strips, and fries along with endless ice cream treats. Jerry, who worked full-time as a cook, was always in the back and rarely spoke to the girls. Even though he was middle-aged, he seemed shy around the younger girls. But having him there made the girls feel safer in the evenings.

As it drew closer to closing time, both girls' phones buzzed. Maddie ignored hers, keeping busy cleaning the tables and restocking supplies. Livie found her in the back room, looking pale.

"Have you checked your messages?" Livie asked.

Maddie frowned. "No. What's going on?"

"It's Caden," Livie said in a shaky voice.

"What's he doing now?" Maddie asked, annoyed.

"He's been in a bad accident," Livie said. "He's been rushed to the hospital. Aaron has been trying to get a hold of you. He texted me."

Maddie stopped what she was doing and stared at Livie with wide eyes. "What?"

"I guess he's not doing too well. He's going into surgery," Livie said. "Aaron asked if you could come to the hospital."

Maddie's heart clenched. This was real. Caden was badly hurt. "I need to go," she said, pulling off her apron. She grabbed her bag, then remembered she didn't have a car.

Jerry had overheard the conversation. "Livie. Drive Maddie to the hospital. I can close up tonight."

Livie nodded and grabbed her things from the back. They both rushed out to Livie's little car and headed to the hospital, which was across town.

As Livie drove, Maddie checked her messages. She had two from Aaron and five from her mother. She quickly dialed her mom's phone.

"Are you okay?" Sandy asked, panic filling her voice. "We just heard about Caden."

"I'm fine," Maddie said, shocked they'd already heard. "Livie is driving me to the hospital now to see Caden."

"Oh, thank goodness." Sandy sighed. "I was scared to death you had been in the truck with Caden. We're heading to the hospital, too. We'll see you there."

Maddie hung up, wondering how her parents had heard about the accident already. She read Aaron's texts, but all they said was that Caden was in an accident. Maddie wondered if Caden had gone to that drinking party and then tried to drive home. She hoped not.

Fifteen minutes later, they arrived at the hospital and entered the emergency room. Caden's parents were already there, along with Aaron and his parents. Livie walked up to Aaron and hugged him, and Maddie did, too.

"Have you heard anything yet?" Maddie asked Aaron.

He shook his head. "You should ask his parents. They were told what was wrong."

Maddie barely knew Caden's parents, but she assumed they knew who she was. She approached them tentatively. "I'm Maddie," she said to the tall, dark-haired woman and even taller brown-haired man. They looked to be the same age as her parents, and Maddie knew immediately where Caden had gotten his wavy brown hair. His father looked just like him.

"Oh, Maddie," Mrs. Addams said, pulling her into a hug. She held on to Maddie for a long time as Maddie's heart broke for her. "I'm glad you're here," she said, finally pulling away.

"It's nice to finally meet you, Maddie," Mr. Addams said. "We were thankful you weren't in the pick-up with Caden when we heard about the accident."

"I was at work," Maddie said, feeling at a loss for words. "Have you heard how he's doing?"

Tears fell down Mrs. Addams' face. "He was pretty banged up," she said softly. "They said he has a punctured lung and a broken leg. He's in surgery now, for the lung."

"Oh, my goodness!" Maddie wrapped her arms around herself.

"The police officer who was the first on the scene said Caden rolled the truck into a ditch, and if Aaron hadn't been following behind him, he might not have been found so quickly. They were out on a dirt road," Mr. Addams said, looking grim. "Aaron said they'd been at a friend's cabin, and he followed Caden home."

Maddie looked across the room at Aaron, who was sitting beside Livie. He had his head in his hands, and Livie had her arm around him. As she watched them, she wondered when the two had become so close.

"Maddie? Do you know where Caden went tonight?" Mrs. Addams asked, wiping her tears.

Maddie's eyes returned to Caden's parents. "He said something about meeting friends at a cabin somewhere, but since I was working, I didn't go," she said. She didn't want to mention that it was a party and get Caden into more trouble than he already was.

"It sounds like it was a drinking party," Mr. Addams said grimly. "The officer said he could smell alcohol on Caden. Aaron tested negative for alcohol, though."

"I don't understand," Mrs. Addams said. "Caden never does stuff like this. He's always home at a decent time or at least calls us."

Maddie was stunned by her words. From what Maddie had seen, Caden runs around at all hours of the night without telling his parents.

"There you are!" Maddie's mother and father came up to her and hugged her tightly. "I was so scared," Sandy said. "Thank goodness you were working."

"I'm fine, Mom," Maddie said, pulling away. "These are Caden's parents. They were just telling me what happened."

The four adults stood in a circle, talking, and Maddie watched as her mother hugged Mrs. Addams as if they were old friends. It felt strange to Maddie that she and Caden had been dating for over a year, and yet she barely knew his parents. She walked over to Livie and Aaron and sat down.

"What happened?" Maddie asked Aaron softly.

Aaron looked up to make sure the parents weren't listening, then turned back to Maddie. His face was drawn, and he had dark circles under his eyes. "Caden drank too much again. I tried to get him to let me drive him home, but he got belligerent. So, I followed him on the dirt road, but he was driving like a crazy person. He was going too fast, then skidded on some gravel and spun out, then rolled."

"That's awful!" Maddie said.

"I was so scared," Aaron said. "I went to him and realized I shouldn't touch him because he was badly hurt, so I called 911. He was passed out, and as far as I know, didn't wake up before surgery."

"He shouldn't have gone to that party," Maddie said, suddenly angry. "You shouldn't have either, but thank goodness you were driving behind him."

"I never intended to drink at the party," Aaron said. "I can't risk getting kicked off the football team my senior year. I just wanted to hang out with some friends and have fun. But Caden took it too far, like he always does. It's like he has a death wish."

Aaron's words hit Maddie hard. She was the reason Caden was upset that evening, and she figured he'd gone to the party to spite her.

"Will you get in trouble with the police?" Livie asked, looking concerned.

Aaron shrugged. "I don't know. They asked me several times where the party was, but I just played dumb. I said I followed Caden out there and back again, and that I wasn't paying attention. They're not buying it, though."

"You should tell them the truth," Maddie said. "Since you weren't drinking, you won't get into trouble."

"Yeah, but everyone in high school will call me a narc if I tell," Aaron said. "I can't do that to the other kids. Some are in football, others are in hockey. Some of the girls there are cheerleaders. We'd all be kicked out of our activities if I told the truth."

Maddie sighed. Every one of them had something to lose. Nearly all the kids entering senior year were hoping for a sports or academic scholarship to help them pay for college. That was a lot of pressure for a seventeen-year-old.

Sandy came up to the kids, and they went silent. "Maddie. We're heading home. Why don't you come with us?"

"I'd like to stay until Caden is out of surgery," Maddie said.

"I'll be staying, too," Aaron said. Livie nodded that she was staying, too.

"I don't know," Sandy said. She looked over at her husband, who gave her a slight nod. "Well, okay. But how will you get home?"

"I'll drive her," Livie said. "I promise we'll be careful."

Sandy nodded and pulled Maddie into a hug. "I'm so glad you weren't in that truck," she whispered to Maddie, aware that Caden's parents were just a few feet away. "I'll see you tomorrow morning."

Maddie hugged her mother back, then her father, and watched as they left the waiting room.

Maddie, Aaron, and Livie walked over to where the Addamses were sitting and sat beside them. Mrs. Addams reached for Maddie's hand.

"Thanks for staying. Caden will appreciate it," Mrs. Addams said.

It was a long night. The three teens scrunched down in their seats, and each finally fell asleep. At three in the morning, Mrs. Addams woke them up.

"He's out of surgery but still sleeping," she told them. "Why don't you three go home and come back to see Caden in the morning. There's nothing you can do for him right now."

Sleepily, Maddie, Livie, and Aaron stood, and each one hugged Mrs. Addams goodbye. They walked silently to their cars.

"Will life ever feel normal again?" Aaron asked the girls. "I feel like everything changed tonight."

Livie hugged Aaron, and Maddie did, too. "Get some sleep," Maddie said. "Tomorrow you'll feel better."

Livie drove Maddie home, and she walked into her silent house. All was dark except for the light over the oven. Maddie quietly went upstairs and fell on her bed. So much had happened since she'd sat here hours before. She closed her eyes and was immediately asleep.

CHAPTER ELEVEN

Maddie

Maddie awoke the next morning at ten. As all the memories of the night before rushed back, she jumped out of bed and grabbed her phone.

"Any news about Caden?" she texted Aaron.

"He's awake, but groggy. His mother texted me. I'll be going over there soon."

Maddie quickly showered, dressed, and headed downstairs. Her sister was in the living room playing a video game, and her mother was sitting at the kitchen counter.

"Do you want some breakfast?" Sandy asked.

"No. I'll have a banana or something," Maddie told her. "Caden is awake, so I want to go see him."

Sandy nodded. "Okay. Let us know how he's doing."

Maddie grabbed a banana off the counter and picked up her mother's keys. "Will you need these today?"

"I can use the Jeep," Sandy said.

Maddie stopped and stared at her mother. There was something about the tone of her voice that didn't seem right.

"What's going on?"

Sandy looked up at her daughter. "Nothing. I'm just..." she hesitated.

"What?" Maddie asked.

"I'm just trying to get over the scare I had last night," Sandy said, her shoulders sagging. "For an instant, I thought you were in the truck with Caden. I'm sorry he was hurt, but I'm also thankful you hadn't gone to the party with him."

"You knew I was at work," Maddie said.

"I realized that, after a moment of fright." Sandy looked her in the eye. "Does Caden drink often? Is that typical of him?"

Maddie wasn't sure how to answer. She didn't want to get Caden into even more trouble, but she also didn't want to lie to her mother. "He does sometimes. You know, like teens do."

"Do you go out drinking with him?" Sandy asked.

Maddie took a breath. "I haven't been anywhere with Caden since summer started," she said. "Because I'm always working. So, no. I don't go out drinking with him." She sounded angrier than she'd meant to. But all the stress of the summer and Caden's accident was wearing on her.

"I'm not trying to upset you, Mads," Sandy said gently. "I'm trying to figure things out. Caden's parents didn't seem to know him at all. When I mentioned your car crashing into a tree, they said they hadn't heard about it. Both of his parents looked surprised, then said they hoped you were okay after the accident. They thought you had crashed it."

This didn't surprise Maddie. She knew Caden wouldn't have told his parents. "Did you tell them Caden did it?"

Sandy shook her head. "No, but your father said afterward that I should have. They need to know their son is irresponsible. But I don't think it's up to us to tell them that."

"I've got to go," Maddie said, moving toward the kitchen door. "I'll be back later. I have a couple of mowing jobs to do."

"Okay. I'll see you later," Sandy said.

On the drive to the hospital, Maddie pondered what her mother had said. It upset her that her mother said Caden was irresponsible, but on the other hand, Maddie already knew he was. But she felt guilty. Maybe if she hadn't fought with Caden, he wouldn't have gone to the party and drank so much. It weighed heavily on her.

Once at the hospital, she checked in with the receptionist and learned that Caden was still in Intensive Care. She was allowed to go up to the ICU but not allowed to go into his room unless one of his parents approved it. Five minutes after arriving, Mrs. Addams came out of the room and led Maddie inside.

"We're only allowed two visitors at a time," Mrs. Addams said. "So, his father went to get coffee so I could bring you in to see Caden."

"How's he doing?" Maddie asked quietly. The place was silent, except for the monitors beeping everywhere, and Maddie felt like she had to whisper.

"He's over the worst," Mrs. Addams said. "They want to monitor him another day before placing him in a regular room. But the doctor said he'd be recuperating in the hospital for a while."

"So, he's going to be okay?" Maddie asked hopefully.

Mrs. Addams smiled. "Yes. But he's pretty banged up, so be prepared."

They walked into Caden's room, and Maddie was shocked at how bad he looked. His face was swollen and black and blue, and he had bandages around his head. His leg was in a cast, and he had a machine beeping with every heartbeat. Luckily, Caden was sleeping because if he'd seen Maddie's expression, he'd have been frightened.

"I'll give you a little time alone," Mrs. Addams said. "He's in and out of it a lot. When Aaron comes, I'll send him up, too."

Maddie nodded, and then she was left alone with Caden.

Sitting down in the chair beside Caden's bed, she was at a loss as to what to do. Should she talk to see if he was awake or let him wake up naturally? Caden must have sensed someone was there because his eyes fluttered open. When he finally focused on Maddie, he tried to smile, then winced.

"Hi," he said in a raspy voice.

"Hi," Maddie said, smiling. "I'd ask how you feel, but it's pretty obvious the answer is not good."

Caden gave a little laugh, then winced again. "It hurts to move, even with the painkillers," he said. "It hurts to breathe, too. I really screwed up this time, Mads."

"You did," she agreed, but grinned. "But you're still here, and that's a good thing."

Caden fell asleep again after that. Aaron came in, and they talked quietly until Caden woke up again. Maddie told Caden she had to go to work for a while but would drop by later. She didn't want to stay too long because she knew Caden's mom and dad would like to be there with him, too.

By the time Maddie got home, she was already exhausted. Her mom and sister had left—probably to go to gymnastics—so she changed into old clothes and drove the lawn mower down the street to the neighbor's yard. When she'd finished both lawns, her phone buzzed. She glanced at it but didn't recognize the number. But she answered in case it was Caden's mom or dad.

"Hello?"

"Maddie? This is Eva," the older woman said, her voice sounding unsure.

Maddie's heart beat faster. Eva had never called her before. What if something had happened to her or Ginny? "Is everything okay?"

"Oh, dear. I called to ask you the same question," Eva said. "We read in the paper that your young man was in an accident, and I wanted to see how you were."

"Oh." Maddie sighed with relief. "That's nice of you. I'm fine. He's not doing so well, but he'll be okay eventually."

"Are you busy? Ginny said to invite you to lunch if you're free," Eva said.

Maddie was surprised. Ginny had a soft heart after all. "I've just finished mowing the neighbor's yard, so I can be right over. Thanks."

"We'll see you then, dear." Eva hung up.

Maddie rode her lawnmower down the long driveway, wondering why the ladies had invited her over. Maybe they wanted to make sure she hadn't been in the truck that night. Whatever the reason, she was glad they wanted her to come over.

"Hi," Maddie said when Eva answered the door. She was wearing one of her long, flowing skirts, this one in turquoise, and a soft, white blouse. Turquoise earrings hung from her ears with a matching necklace around her neck.

"Maddie. I'm so glad you came," Eva said, hugging her. "Ginny is making your favorite grilled cheese sandwiches, and she knew you wouldn't want to miss them."

"It smells wonderful," Maddie said, slipping off her shoes.

They walked around through the living room to the table,

and Ginny looked up at them from her spot at the counter.

"Well, you look all in one piece, thank goodness," Ginny said matter-of-factly. "I'm guessing you weren't in the truck with your beau."

"Is that why you invited me? To make sure I was still alive?" Maddie teased.

Ginny turned red. "It was Eva's idea," she muttered, returning to her work.

"Come, dear," Eva said. "Sit and tell us how your young man is. Was he hurt badly?"

Maddie told the ladies about Caden's injuries and how the accident happened, leaving out the fact that he'd been drinking. She'd already told them once before he was considered a 'bad boy,' so she didn't want to make him sound worse. Both women shook their heads in sympathy and said they were glad to hear he would heal from his injuries.

Ginny served the sandwiches along with chips and ranch dip. The three of them took a few bites before Eva spoke again.

"I'm so happy you weren't in the accident," she said. "But are you okay? It must have been a shock for you to have this happen to your boyfriend."

Maddie paused as she was about to take another bite of her sandwich. Eva was the only person who'd thought to ask how she was feeling. Tears suddenly filled her eyes, and she reached for her napkin to wipe them away.

"That's so nice of you to ask," Maddie said, her voice trembling. "It has been hard. I was so scared last night, waiting at the hospital, and then today, seeing him was tough."

Eva nodded and patted her arm. "I completely understand. I'm sure you were trying to be strong for his parents and your other friends and didn't acknowledge that you were hurting, too."

"You're right. I've been so stressed lately, and then this happened. I know I don't have the right to think about myself when he's hurting, but it's been hard," Maddie said.

"You have every right to have your own feelings," Ginny said.

Maddie took a breath. "The problem is, he and I fought right before he drove off. I blame myself for his going to the party and driving recklessly. I've just been so upset lately, and I think I took it out on him." Tears filled her eyes again.

Eva looked at her tenderly. "Dear, none of this is your fault. He chose to drive recklessly. You didn't make him do that. You can't place all this on yourself. Believe me, I know."

"How did you stand all the pressure on you when you were studying to be a dancer?" Maddie asked. "You were one hundred percent committed to your art, but wasn't it hard? All of my friends are going through the same thing as me. We're trying to figure out our next step in life, and we're not even out of high school yet.

Eva nodded. "It was different for me. I knew from the time I was a young child that I wanted to dance. That was my entire focus. Sure, I still had to go to school, plus study dance. And it wasn't always easy. But I put the pressure on myself; no one else did. My mother said I could quit any time I wanted, but I didn't want to. I wanted to dance. I wanted to dance for Mr. Balanchine."

Chapter Twelve

Eva – 1946

Eva learned to dance in her pointe shoes slowly, but with perfection. Once she found her balance, she was able to move easily on pointe. Her friend, Mary, moved up to pointe class, too, but didn't find it as easy. Eva spent many afternoons after class with her, showing her how to tighten her gluteal muscles to balance, but Mary couldn't get the hang of it.

"It'll come to you eventually," Eva told her pretty blond friend. "You've done so well so far. I know you can master this."

But each day in class, Mme Doubrovska approached Mary and quietly showed her how to stand or move her feet correctly. "Bend those arches," she'd tell Mary. "They must be strong to stay up on pointe."

Mary said she felt she was being admonished, and she hated class. But Eva told her that Mme Doubrovska was only trying to help her.

"She repositions my feet, too," Eva said. "And my arms, and everything else. You're not the only one." But Eva knew that wasn't true. Mme Doubrovska corrected Mary more often than any of the other students.

One afternoon, about a year after Eva had started pointe class, Mr. B came to watch the girls. He spoke softly to Mme Doubrovska, then left. After class, Madame called Eva aside.

"Mr. Balanchine would like you to move up into the elite dancers' class," she told her, smiling. "I teach that class as well. The girls always wear their pointe shoes in class. The class is every day after pointe class."

Eva's heart leapt. She knew that only students who showed the most promise of becoming NYCB dancers were invited to join the class. "Thank you," she told Mme Doubrovska.

The older teacher smiled. "Dear, you've earned it. Mr. B sees something in you to move you up. Work hard, and you'll do well."

Instead of changing, Eva kept her pointe shoes on and walked toward the door to go to the other studio. Mary caught up with her at the door.

"What did Mme Doubrovska say to you?" Mary asked.

Eva felt bad because she knew this would hurt her friend. But she couldn't lie. "Mr. B has asked me to join the advance class after pointe class."

Mary's mouth dropped open. "Oh, you're so lucky. I've always known you were better than all of us. I'll never get invited to that class. I should just quit." Tears filled her eyes.

"No, Mary," Eva said. "You can't quit. You've worked so hard. Many students who were never invited to join the advanced class were still taken on by the NYCB. And you might still get invited over the next few months."

Mary wiped her tears. "It feels so useless," she said. "You're only fourteen, but you'll be in with the older students. I should be that good by now."

"I'm sorry," Eva said. "I have to go to class, but meet me afterward, and we can go to the automat and talk, okay?"

Mary nodded, then turned and walked down the hallway.

Eva rushed to class and found an open spot at the barre. All the girls were older than her and much taller. There were boys in the class as well, but the girls all wore pointe shoes. Mme Doubrovska was at the head of the class, waiting for the last of the students to arrive. Finally, when the pianist began to play, she called out to start in first position, and the class began.

At first, Eva was able to keep up because it was like a regular class. They did pliés and relevés in first, second, and fifth position. Then, they faced the barre as Madame called, "Plié, echappé, plié, straight. Plié, relevé, plié straight." Eva kept up, but the tempo increased, and they moved their feet faster. Now, Eva knew why this was the advanced class. Everything they were learning was the basics—only quicker.

Eva did her best to keep up, but by the time they did tendu exercises in first position, she was exhausted. Madame called out, "Front, side, back, first. Front, side, back, first." As she followed along, the tempo quickened. Eva had to stop a few times because she'd lost her spot, then start again. But she didn't give up.

After class, Eva stretched longer than usual because she feared her muscles would bunch up. The other girls had packed up and left by the time Eva took off her pointe shoes and packed her bag.

Mme Doubrovska came to stand over her. "You did just fine for your first class, Eva. It's a difficult class, but I know you will catch up quickly."

Eva felt like she was going to cry. Holding back tears, she said, "I felt like I was so far behind. Everything is so fast."

The older woman smiled down at her. "If you are to dance for Mr. Balanchine, you must learn to be very fast. His dances are created with quick beats and swift movements. It takes time, but you will be fine, dear."

"Thank you, Madame," Eva said, standing up. "I'll work hard, I promise."

It was late by the time Eva left the classroom, and she suddenly remembered she'd told Mary to meet her after class. But when she looked around for her, she wasn't there. Rehearsals were going on in the other studios, but Mary was nowhere to be found.

Once she arrived home, Eva was happy to see her mother there and cooking dinner.

"Oh, honey," Gwen said, stirring something on the stove. "I had a craving for tomato soup and grilled cheese sandwiches. Are you hungry?"

"Starved," Eva said. As she helped her mother butter the bread and place it on the griddle with thick slices of cheese inside, she told her about her day.

"That's wonderful!" Gwen said happily. "You are on track to becoming a ballerina. I'm so proud of you."

Eva was happy her mother was pleased. Dancing had become so much a part of her life that she expected so much of herself. But her mother congratulated her every step of the way. "I'm afraid Mary is feeling down about not being selected to attend the advanced class," she told her mother as they sat down to eat. "I feel bad."

"I'm sorry to hear she was disappointed, dear," Gwen said. "But it's not your fault that you are succeeding and she isn't. She still has plenty of time to move forward if she works hard."

"I know," Eva said. "But I want her to be happy, too."

"Oh, honey." Gwen set her sandwich down and looked at her. "I'm glad you want good things for your friend, but we can only cheer other people on. You have no control over whether or not she'll become a dancer. That's in her hands alone."

Eva nodded. On some level, she understood. But she did wish for everyone to succeed.

As the months went by, Eva did succeed in keeping up with the advanced class. She tried to control her steps so she'd not only be fast but also precise. She'd watched Mr. B often tell the dancers in rehearsals to be quick, but precise. No sloppy feet. Eva knew it would take time for her to excel at both, but she worked hard.

After turning fifteen, Eva was told she could now attend adagio class as well. They had her drop one of her basic classes, so she only had class once a day. Then she had pointe class, the advanced class, and adagio. Adagio class was taught by one of the NYCB's principal male dancers, Jacques d'Amboise, a handsome man with a square jaw and gorgeous dark hair. All the girls had a crush on him, and Eva understood why. He was also kind and patient as he taught the boys in the class how to support the girls as they spun, leapt, and moved about.

Eva loved Adagio class. It was the first time she'd worked alongside boys her age and older. Until now, she hadn't even thought about the opposite sex, but being with these young men, day after day, she found herself developing crushes on a few of them. But she kept her thoughts to herself.

Eva had no one to confide in anymore. She could no longer talk to Mary, who'd been her best friend since she'd started dance school. Mary had become sullen and jealous over Eva's quick rise in the advanced classes. It made Eva sad, but, as her mother had said, there was nothing she could do about how

Mary felt. Still, she missed having a best friend.

Eva knew Mr. B kept tabs on her progress, and he contin-ued to offer her scholarships so she could study at SAB. Occa-sionally, she was given small parts in larger ballets, like *The Nutcracker,* when they needed a large cast. The more she performed, the less fearful she became of being on stage.

Eva's home life was still as hectic as her life at SAB. Her mother was doing well at her job after being there for two years. Gwen also began dating a new real estate partner who'd joined the firm, Raymond Mandel. Ray was twenty years older than Gwen, but he was a kind man and nice to her mother. Many nights when Eva arrived home, her mother was out. But Eva didn't mind. She was happy her mother had finally found a nice man she could spend time with.

Just after Eva turned sixteen in March of 1958, she and her mother moved into a bigger apartment in the same building. They moved one floor down and had a bedroom along with a slightly bigger living room, dining room, and kitchen. It felt like a castle to the two women who'd lived in one-room apart-ments for years, even if they had to share a bedroom.

Late one afternoon, Eva found an empty studio to practice in after her classes were over. She loved dancing on pointe, but she knew that, to someday be accepted into the NYCB, she had to excel at it. So, while the older dancers rehearsed in the studios down the hall, she'd often come to the smaller studio and practice.

After warming up at the barre, Eva stood in the middle of the floor and practiced her pirouettes, bourrées, and jumps. She wanted to learn to do her steps quickly and precisely, just as Mr. B expected of his dancers.

Hearing the rehearsal music through the walls, Eva began

improvising a dance, spinning, balancing on one leg, and making tiny bourrée steps across the floor. She moved her head and arms gracefully to the music along with the footwork. From one corner of the room, she ran four steps and leaped into the air, her legs perfectly positioned, her arms reaching gracefully as she'd seen the other dancers do many times. But as she came down on the floor and took a sweeping bow, her eyes landed on Mr. B, standing in the doorway, smiling.

Embarrassed, Eva stood up quickly. "I didn't know you were there."

"I can be quiet as a cat," he said, chuckling. Everyone in the school knew that Mr. B loved cats and owned a few.

"I was practicing," Eva said, feeling the need to explain why she was there.

"You were dancing," Mr. B corrected her. "What dance were you performing?"

"I was making up steps to the music I overheard from the other room."

Mr. B moved closer and tilted his head. "Ah. You were choreographing your own ballet. Are you trying to take my job?"

Eva could tell from the amused look on his face that he was teasing. "Never," she said with a smile. "No one could replace you."

He waved his hand through the air. "Anyone could replace me. Show me your dance again. I'd like to see it."

"I don't remember what I did. I was just improvising," Eva said.

"How do you think ballets are created? I improvise until I find the perfect combinations," Mr. B said, coming up in front of her. He was wearing his usual cowboy-style shirt with a scarf around his neck, slacks, and jazz shoes.

"Okay." She closed her eyes and listened to the music, feeling its beat. It was a classical song, and she could see the steps in her mind. Eva began with a glissade to the right, then to the left, back and forth, then went up on pointe into tiny bourrée steps across the floor. She stopped in fourth position, then did three perfect pirouettes, coming to a stop in fourth position, pointing her right foot and bowing over it, as she'd seen dancers do on stage. When she finished, she stood and looked at Mr. B, feeling embarrassed.

"Beautiful," he said, looking pleased. "Now, let's try the pirouettes with me spotting you and then have you stop in a high arabesque while you hold my arm for support."

Eva blinked. He wanted to dance with her? "Should I start from the beginning?"

"No, no. I think you should start with a deep fourth position so you can spin faster," he said. "I'll show you." He placed his legs into fourth position, then moved his front foot even farther out. Then, with his arms circled for momentum, Mr. B spun on demi-pointe. "See? You will spin faster."

Eva tried while Mr. B stood close to her, his hands circling her waist but not touching her, just as the young men did in adagio class. Placing her feet into a deep fourth position, she spun, getting more momentum than she had with a smaller fourth position. After three spins, she stopped, her foot flat on the ground, then went back up into a beautiful arabesque, her right foot on pointe and her left leg held high in the air. Mr. B held on to her expertly, moving gracefully in front of her so she could hold onto his arm.

"Brava!" Mr. B said, smiling widely. "Let's dance some more."

For almost an hour, Mr. B instructed her through several dance steps as he assisted. He asked her what she thought, then told her to try something on her own. It felt like she was playing the part of a principal ballerina, except she was also helping to create the steps. It was exhilarating.

"Very good," Mr. B said when they were finished. "I believe we've created my next ballet."

"Is this how you create a ballet?" she asked, her heart still pounding from working so hard.

"Yes. It's much easier to have the dancers with me, and we create the steps as we go along. You listen well. And you are far more advanced with your steps than I'd realized." Mr. B smiled. "But it is late, and we should walk you home. Do you still live in the direction of my apartment?"

Eva nodded. She sat on the floor, took off her pointe shoes, then pulled on a pair of slacks over her tights. Slipping on her shoes and coat, she picked up her bag. It was still cold at night in New York, and she made sure to dress warm.

"I will walk you partway," Mr. B said. He allowed her to go through the door first, and followed her down the hallway, where he entered his office to put on his coat and change into street shoes. Soon, they were outside, walking down the quiet street.

"Are you interested in dancing for the company?" Mr. B asked, looking at her inquisitively.

"Oh, yes," Eva said. "That's all I've ever wanted to do."

"How are you doing at regular school? Are you keeping up with your studies?"

"Yes," Eva said. "School has always been easy for me. I have two years left."

"Good. Good. We want our dancers to finish high school.

It is important," Mr. B said.

They walked in silence to his apartment building, then stopped in front. "Will you be okay to get home from here?" he asked, looking concerned.

"I'll be fine, thank you," Eva said. "I do this every night."

He grinned. "You are a hard worker, Eva. I do believe you will do well."

"Thank you, Mr. B. Goodnight."

"Goodnight, dear."

She walked away, aware he was watching her, her heart still beating fast. Even though she'd known Mr. B since she was ten, they had never spoken as much as tonight. She was thrilled that he thought she was a good dancer, and she'd had a chance to see how he created his ballets.

The next day, Betty approached Eva before her first afternoon class. "Mr. Balanchine would like you to join his ballet company."

Eva nearly fainted. At sixteen, she was being asked to dance for the New York City Ballet.

CHAPTER THIRTEEN

Maddie

Maddie couldn't stop thinking about Eva's story long after she'd returned home and headed to the hospital to see Caden. Eva had understood Maddie's feelings of guilt over Caden's accident. Eva had experienced the same thing, feeling guilty for excelling at dance while her friend, Mary, wasn't. Mary falling behind was not Eva's fault, as Caden's accident was not Maddie's fault. Still, it was hard not to blame herself.

When Maddie arrived at the hospital, Caden was awake and less groggy. His parents had gone home for a while, so she was alone with him. As she entered, Caden sighed.

"Good. A familiar face," he said.

"Have you had a lot of visitors?" Maddie asked.

"The police were here a little while ago," Caden said. "Aaron had texted my parents to warn us they were coming here. They kept asking me where the party was and who had supplied minors with alcohol. I told them that I didn't remember the address. It was out on a lake south of town, and I didn't know who was putting the party on."

"Did they believe you?" Maddie asked, suspecting that they hadn't.

"They have no choice but to believe me," Caden said. "I'm not narcing on my friends, and neither is Aaron. He told them he followed me to the house and didn't know the address either. I said I was told which lake and followed the road until I saw a bunch of cars."

Maddie sighed. She understood not telling on his friends, but these people were putting young people's lives in danger. "Are they going to charge you with drunk driving?"

Caden shrugged, then winced. "I have to remember not to shrug," he said, half-teasing, half-serious. "They keep threatening me with arrest, but there's not much they can do. I'd pay a fine, lose my license until I'm eighteen, and have to take driving classes. Once I'm eighteen, I can get my license back, and that's that."

Maddie sat back in her chair. It unnerved her that Caden wasn't taking all this seriously. "But after all this, I hope you'll think twice about drinking and driving. You could have died."

"Well, I didn't," Caden said.

"But you could have," Maddie said more forcefully.

Caden rolled his eyes. "You sound like my mother."

His insolent tone hit a nerve. Maddie stood. "I need to go. I have to work at the Freeze tonight."

"Why are you mad?" Caden asked, frowning. "This didn't happen to you; it happened to me."

Maddie glared at him. "It happened to everyone who cares about you. Don't you understand that? We were all scared to death that you might die. And now, you're acting like it was nothing. But it was something. Something big. Think about that." She spun and stormed out of the room.

Sitting in her car in the hospital parking lot, Maddie called Livie.

"Hi, Mads," Livie said. "What's up?"

"Are you working at the Freeze tonight?" Maddie asked. "I could really use a friend right now."

"No, I'm not," Livie said. "My gymnastics competition in Minneapolis was today. We're driving home now."

"Oh, I'm so sorry I forgot," Maddie said. She suddenly felt terrible keeping Livie up late last night because of Caden's accident. "How did you do?"

"I did great! I placed first in two of my three categories and second in the other. A coach from the University of Denver was there and talked to me for a while. I guess I have two options for college now," Livie said.

"That's wonderful! I'm so happy for you," Maddie said. "I'm so sorry I forgot and kept you up late last night. You should have said something."

"It's okay, Mads," Livie said. "My parents drove me to the competition, so I slept on the way down there. All is good."

"Well, I'm glad you did so well," Maddie said.

"Thanks. I'll drive by tonight when we get home and show you my medals," Livie said.

"Great. See you then." Maddie hung up and sighed. If Livie wasn't working tonight, that meant that crabby Carrie was working.

Maddie drove home, ate a quick frozen meal she'd heated up in the microwave, then left again to go to work. It was only four-thirty, but it felt like midnight already because she was so beat. She pulled into the busy parking lot, parked, and walked inside.

"Hurry up," Carrie barked at her. "Can't you see I'm

swamped here?"

Maddie ignored her and went in back to put her purse away and put on her apron. She waved to Jerry, who was busy cooking. "Thanks for last night," she yelled over the fryers.

He smiled and nodded. "Hope he's okay."

"He's doing better. Thanks," Maddie said. She hurried to the counter and began filling orders from the long line of customers.

"Took you long enough," Carrie said, looking frazzled. Her dark hair was falling out of its ponytail, and her apron was stained.

"I came on time for my shift," Maddie said quietly as she handed cones to two young children.

"Whatever," Carrie said.

They were busy for an hour, and then it finally slowed down. Maddie went out to the dining area and wiped down tables. When she returned behind the counter, Carrie nearly growled at her. "Fill the cones and cups. They're almost empty."

Maddie glared at her. "Change your apron. You look like a short-order cook at a greasy spoon."

Carrie stopped and stared at her, looking stunned that Maddie would talk back to her. Then she looked down at her apron. Her laughter came as much as a surprise to Carrie as it did to Maddie.

"You're right. I'm filthy." She grinned.

Maddie stared at her like she'd gone insane. "You laughed. I yelled at you, and you laughed."

"It was funny," Carrie said, wiping her forehead with the back of her arm. "You've never talked back to me before."

"And you find that funny?"

"Yeah," Carrie said. "I thought you were too goody-goody

to talk back. I guess you have some backbone after all." She left to change her apron.

Maddie stared after her. What was wrong with Carrie? She had to yell at her for her to be nice?

"Why were you alone?" Maddie asked after Carrie returned. "Someone was supposed to work with you until I came on."

"She called in sick at the last minute," Carrie said. "High school girls. You can't trust them to work."

"Hey!" Maddie said.

Carrie smiled. "Okay, some high school girls. You're always on time."

"Better," Maddie said, smiling.

As they worked putting the place back in order, Maddie told Carrie about Caden's accident.

"I heard about the accident," Carrie said. "I didn't know it was him. I'm glad he's okay, but quite frankly, he's a jerk. You can do better. Way better."

Maddie wanted to defend Caden, but she couldn't. Carrie was right, he'd been a jerk the last few months.

Livie showed up later that evening with her medals in hand.

"Congratulations!" Maddie said. "And now you have another choice for college. That's great."

"Wow! You won these?" Carrie asked. "That's so great."

Livie stared at Carrie like she had two heads. "Uh, thanks."

"I knew you were in gymnastics, but I hadn't realized you were doing so well. Super cool." Carrie walked to the back to help Jerry clean the grills.

Livie stared at Maddie and whispered. "What happened to Carrie? Is she sick?"

Maddie laughed. "No. She's human after all."

Maddie went directly home after they closed. She was

exhausted from her long day, and because she hadn't slept much the night before. She thought about texting Caden, then thought better of it. She was still mad at him. Was he really that immature to think what had happened to him was not a big deal?

It was ten thirty by the time she arrived home, and no one was up. So, she turned off the kitchen lights and walked up to her room. After changing into a long T-shirt, Maddie suddenly felt wide awake, so she pulled out the notebook she'd been writing Eva's story in and started writing more of her story.

Eva had been asked to join Mr. Balanchine's ballet company. That had been huge. Maddie couldn't imagine being asked to do such a thing at only sixteen. Here she was, a year older than that, and she still didn't know where she wanted to go to school. But Eva already had her life planned out for her by the age of sixteen.

Maddie wondered if it was because people were more mature in their teens back then, or if it was just Eva who seemed mature?

The next day, Maddie didn't have to work, so she went to the hospital late in the morning to see Caden. He'd been moved to a regular room, and he could have more visitors. When she arrived, he was alone, sitting up in bed, eating his lunch.

"I thought you were mad at me," Caden said, sulking.

"I am. But I'm still concerned about how you're doing." Maddie sat in the chair near the bed.

"Well, everyone is mad at me, so you might as well be, too." Caden took a bite of his sandwich and chewed slowly.

"Who else is mad?"

"My parents. Aaron. Pretty much everyone I know," Caden said. "You're all taking this so seriously. Accidents happen, that's why they call them accidents."

"What happened to you was a self-inflicted accident," Maddie said. "You chose to drive drunk, and you rolled your truck. It wouldn't have happened if you'd been sober."

"Gees, Mads. What are you? Thirty? So, I drank a little. Kids do that stuff. At least some of us do, but not you. Not everyone is a goody-goody."

Maddie grew angry. "When did you become so stupid? Or were you always this stupid, and I just ignored it?"

Caden looked her way. "I'm not the one who's changed, Mads. I'm the same person I always was. You're the one who's so afraid to enjoy life."

"There's a difference between enjoying life and ruining your life," Maddie said, standing up. "And you seem bound and determined to ruin yours. Good luck with that." She stormed out of the room and to the elevator. Her heart didn't stop pounding until she was sitting in her mother's car in the parking lot.

The tears finally came. Was this it? Was she finally coming to her senses and breaking up with Caden?

Her phone buzzed, and she ignored it until it buzzed again. Taking a deep breath and wiping her eyes, she looked at it. Her mother was calling.

"Hi," Maddie said, trying to sound normal.

"Hi," her mother said. "I just had a call from Eva, wondering if we'd like to go over there for lunch. Do you want to go?"

Thinking of Eva, Maddie smiled. It was like she always knew when Maddie needed a friend. "Sure. I'm just leaving the hospital."

"Okay. Come to the house first, and we can walk there together."

Maddie checked her mascara to make sure it wasn't running

before driving home. She didn't want to have to explain to her mother why she'd been crying. She parked the car in the driveway and walked into the kitchen, where her mother was waiting.

"Are you two really going to lunch at the witch's house?" Lily asked from the living room.

"They aren't witches," Maddie said firmly. "Don't call them that. They're nice ladies."

"You should come with us to lunch," Sandy said to Lily. "Then you can see for yourself that they are just normal people."

Lily's eyes grew wide, and she shook her head. "No way. You both can be boiled in oil, but not me."

Maddie rolled her eyes while her mother chuckled.

"Come on," Sandy said to her eldest daughter. "Let's go."

They walked the short distance down the quiet neighborhood road toward the house. "Did you see Caden today?" Sandy asked.

"Yes."

"How is he?"

"He's being stupid," Maddie blurted out. "He doesn't think what happened was a big deal. And he's mad because everyone around him is telling him he needs to grow up."

Sandy looked over at Maddie. "What do you think?"

"I know he needs to grow up," Maddie said.

They stopped at the beginning of the long driveway, and they both looked up it.

"When I was a little girl, I loved coming here," Sandy said. "It wasn't scary at all. We all knew that Mlle Arthur was kind, and even though Mrs. Robertson was grumpy, she wasn't scary. I don't know when the rumors began in your generation, but I hated it."

"It's nice you had happy memories here," Maddie said. "But why didn't you ever visit her?"

Sandy sighed. "I did, a few times. But life just got in the way, and as time goes on, you have to leave your childhood dreams behind. I guess it was easier not to come here anymore."

"That's sad," Maddie said.

They followed the driveway to the house and walked up the stairs. Maddie led the way and knocked on the door. It opened immediately.

"Maddie, dear," Eva said, smiling brightly. "I'm so happy you could make it." She glanced around Maddie and saw Sandy, and her smile grew even wider. "Oh, Sandy. It's so good to see you." Eva reached out her arms, and Sandy stepped into them.

"I'm sorry it's been so long," Sandy said, tears falling down her cheeks.

"It feels like it was just yesterday," Eva said softly.

Maddie watched as teacher and student hugged. She felt her own eyes tear up. Maddie never thought of her mother having a life before she was born, let alone being a young woman. She realized now that there was so much she didn't know about her mother.

"Come in and close the door before you let all the flies inside," Ginny said from the kitchen doorway.

Maddie chuckled. Ginny was always the sensible one.

Sandy walked over to Ginny. "It's nice to see you, Mrs. Robertson. And thank you for inviting me to lunch."

"Oh, forget that Mrs. Robertson nonsense," Ginny said. She hugged Sandy, then stood back. "Call me Ginny. My, you haven't changed a bit, have you? Still young and beautiful."

Sandy looked stunned. "Thank you. But I have changed. I have teenage daughters now."

"Well, that might just be the death of you," Ginny said.

Sandy laughed. She walked over to where Maddie and Eva were standing near the table.

Maddie noticed her mother staring at the double doors. Eva noticed, too.

"You want to see the dance room, I can tell," Eva said. "It really hasn't changed a bit. Maddie, dear. Will you do the honors?"

Maddie nodded and pulled open first one door, and then the other. Sun filled the large room from the enormous windows.

Sandy walked slowly inside the room as Eva and Maddie watched. She gazed at the large portraits of Eva dancing, then went over to one of the ballet barres and placed her hands on it.

"You feel it again, don't you?" Eva asked, drawing closer to Sandy. "The desire to dance. It pulls you in, just as it did all those years ago."

Maddie watched as her mother's hands caressed the barre. She saw her reflection in the window. Her mother's face looked dreamy, as if she were remembering all the years she'd spent here, dancing.

Sandy turned around. "Nothing has changed. It's still the same beautiful place."

Eva smiled. "It's still the perfect place to teach ballet. I always dreamed of someone following in my footsteps and continuing dance lessons here. I had hoped that person would be you."

Sandy chuckled. "It was just that. Only a dream. I loved dancing, but there was no future in it."

Eva tilted her head and studied Sandy. "Maybe there still could be. You're young. You could teach ballet evenings and summers."

Sandy shook her head. "Oh, no. I couldn't dance anymore, let alone teach. I've been away from it too long."

"It's like riding a bike, dear," Eva said gently. "Your body never forgets the movements. It would come back to you within days."

Sandy looked skeptical, but continued to walk around the room, as if in a trance.

"Be careful," Ginny said from the doorway. "She'll have you signing up little ballerinas tomorrow if Eva has her way."

Sandy turned and smiled at Ginny. "It would be fun, I'll admit. But it would also be work."

"You'd have to get a new pianist," Ginny said. "My gnarled old fingers won't let me play anymore."

"Or you could use music and speakers," Maddie said. "It's not like a pianist, but it would work."

"That's the spirit," Eva said.

Sandy slowly shook her head. "It sounds lovely, but I wouldn't have the time for it."

Eva's smile faded. "It's something to think about, though."

"Well, let's think about lunch for now before it goes stale," Ginny said, turning away. Sandy walked softly across the dance floor and helped Maddie close the doors, leaving her memories behind them.

"I think you'd love to teach dance," Maddie said quietly to her mother. "You're a teacher, it would come naturally to you."

Sandy studied her daughter for a moment, then dropped her eyes. They all sat at the small table and began eating lunch. Ginny made club wraps and placed cut-up vegetables and dip on the table.

"Tell me more about your story," Maddie said, looking at Eva. "Last time you stopped at being hired by Balanchine to join the New York City Ballet."

Eva smiled. "My whole world changed that day. It was like a dream come true."

"I'd love to hear about it," Sandy said.

"Well, you'll be able to read about it soon," Eva said with a grin. "Maddie is writing my story."

Sandy turned to her daughter. "Really? You're writing about her?"

Maddie suddenly felt embarrassed. "I'm just writing what she's told me."

"And I'm sure it will be wonderful," Eva said. She washed down a bite of her food with a sip of iced tea, then began. "The day after I was asked to join the ballet, everything changed. It was work, but I loved every moment of it. I was getting stronger and becoming a better dancer. But first, I had to learn the roles quickly. There was no time for lollygagging when you worked for the great Mr. B."

CHAPTER FOURTEEN

Eva – 1958

Eva immediately began taking Mr. B's daily class, where he not only taught technique but also worked with dancers rehearsing ballets. She was overwhelmed at first, taking class with the many talented principal and soloist dancers, as well as women who'd been in the corps de ballet for several years. But as she practiced, she lost herself in the music and the steps and tried to put aside her feelings of inadequacy.

Eva took a one-hour class every morning and then had one-hour rehearsal sessions for each ballet she was learning. The performance season was already over, but the dancers never stopped working. They were going on a summer tour of towns through upstate New York, so they had to be ready.

Eva was given small parts in the corps de ballet and told to learn them quickly. She was to dance in five different ballets during their summer tour. Once Mr. B's class was finished, she was off with the other dancers, watching and learning as quickly as she could under the watchful eye of the teachers.

Eva felt like all her dreams had come true—and sooner

than she'd anticipated. She learned small parts in *Stars & Stripes*, *Western Symphony*, *Symphony in C,* and was a background swan in *Swan Lake.* She also played a background fairy in *A Midsummer Night's Dream.* There was so much to practice and learn, but she'd watched these ballets so often, it was easy for her to pick up the steps. And the best part of all, she was now a paid dancer and could help her mother with expenses. That made her the proudest of all.

Working on her schoolwork, however, took a back seat to dancing. Eva was determined to graduate and fulfil Mr. B's request that all his dancers finish high school. But it was hard. She studied in the morning, then began dance class at ten and rehearsed the rest of the day. By evening, she was exhausted.

"How do you like dancing for my little company?" Mr. B asked one night as they both walked down the sidewalk toward home. He'd grinned when he'd said 'little.'

"I love it," Eva replied, knowing full well that Mr. B watched all the dancers closely, keeping tabs on how well they were doing. "I couldn't ask for anything better."

He stopped walking and turned to her. "You mean you wouldn't want to be a soloist or principal dancer?"

Eva stopped, too. "Oh, no. I mean, yes. I'd love to be a soloist or principal dancer. But I'm enjoying learning in the corps so maybe, someday, I can advance to a higher level."

Mr. B laughed. "You are a talented dancer, and you work hard. I don't doubt you will rise to the top soon." He stopped in front of a small café that was still open late at night. "Would you like to have something to eat before going home?"

Eva's heart pounded. She liked Mr. B and respected him greatly. But she'd also heard the rumors of how he fell in love with his dancers. She didn't want to be put in a situation where her relationship with him would become awkward.

"Thank you, but I must get home," she said quickly. "My mother worries when I walk home late at night."

Mr. B studied her for a moment, then nodded. "Of course. We do not want to worry your mother. Go along home. I think I will get a bite to eat." He smiled at her, then walked into the café.

Eva walked the rest of the way home, hoping she hadn't insulted Mr. B. After all the work she'd put into her dancing, she'd be devastated if he fired her.

Fortunately, Eva's worries were for naught. The next day in class, Mr. B treated her the same as he always had. He even asked her to come in front of the class and demonstrate the perfect piqué turn.

"Watch as Eva turns," he told the other dancers. "Her arms move perfectly, while her turns are smooth, as if on air. How lovely it would be if everyone did a piqué turn like this."

It was both embarrassing and exciting for Mr. B to tell the class that her step was perfect. And she was thankful he didn't hold the previous night against her for not joining him.

Of course, the older dancers didn't appreciate being told to dance like the youngest dancer. Several walked by her after class, calling her "Little Miss Piqué." Eva realized immediately that being treated special by Mr. B was not a good thing.

"Don't mind them," Allegra Kent, a principal dancer, said to Eva. "They get jealous easily. You are a talented dancer for your age and have caught Mr. B's eye, and that bothers many of the older dancers."

"Thank you," Eva said, feeling starstruck. But she knew Miss Kent was right. She had to ignore any negative attention and continue doing her very best.

Eva had a wonderful time on the summer tour, but for the first time ever, she realized that dancing on pointe continuously was strenuous and painful. Before, she'd only taken one-hour classes at a time. Now, she was dancing on stage several times a day, and it took a toll on her feet, ankles, and knees.

Like the other dancers, she first put bandages around her toes, wrapped her feet, then stuffed the shoes with anything soft to keep her feet from scraping against the rough parts of the shoes. She found quilt batting worked best, but even that would smash down and eventually hurt. She also tried wads of Kleenex or paper towels, as some of the dancers did. But the pain was always there, and she had to ignore it and dance as if floating on air. It was all a part of being a ballerina.

After the tour, she spent the few weeks off before the fall season visiting Ginny, wandering museums in the city, and practicing daily to keep her strength up. When the new season began, she happily returned to Mr. B's morning class, eager to grow stronger and more disciplined as a dancer.

Balanchine's classes were more about a quick warm-up and then getting to rehearsals. Eva had learned quickly to show up earlier and do extra barre work before Mr. B arrived, so she'd be warmed up and ready to go. Many of the other dancers did that as well, but as the weeks went by, Eva noticed that some didn't attend Mr. B's classes, choosing to attend another teacher's class instead. Eva could see by the look on Mr. B's face that he didn't like that. He expected everyone to dance as **he** taught, and it was an insult to him that they'd choose another class.

"Those of you who show up daily will benefit more than those who disappear by week's end," he said one Friday morning, looking disgruntled. "You will excel quicker."

Eva respected Mr. B for all he'd done for her up to that

point and wouldn't have even thought of missing his class.

Aside from the small parts she'd learned in the spring, she was given the part of a white snowflake in *The Nutcracker*. Much to her surprise, she was also cast as one of the ensemble girls in blue dresses in the ballet, *Serenade*. It was an honor to dance in this sweeping ballet, the first created in America by Mr. Balanchine. Eva was both excited and frightened at the first rehearsal. She'd watched the ballet multiple times and hoped she was able to keep up with the quick music and high kicks. Often, she'd seen the other dancers come off the stage, huffing and puffing for air because the dance was so physical.

Mr. B oversaw the first few rehearsals for that year's *Serenade*. Under his watchful eye, Eva learned the steps, twirling, running, and standing in sweeping arabesques before moving more. When Eva or another dancer missed a step or got lost, Mr. B would only say, "Keep moving. No one in the audience will know you made a mistake. Just keep with the flow of the music."

At one point, as Eva made the many high kicks that would send the tulle skirts flying once they were in costume, Mr. B called her out.

"Eva, dear," he said, stopping the music. "You kick high, but can you hold your leg that high?"

Eva's face turned red, and she was aghast at being made the center of attention. "I'm not sure," she finally answered.

"Come, dear." Mr. B had her leave the group of women and asked her to do her highest kick, but to hold it there and not let it drop.

With a pounding heart, Eva stood in place and swept her leg high into the air, but just as Mr. B suspected, she was unable to hold it that high, and it dropped.

"See," he said kindly. "When we kick, we must do it with control. Only kick as high as you can hold it. It is of no matter if you can't kick as high as another girl, it only matters that your movements are controlled."

Eva nodded, still embarrassed, and ran back to her spot in the group.

"And that applies to all of you," Mr. B said. "No crazy kicks. Controlled kicks only."

The women murmured, then the music began. As Eva danced around the rehearsal studio, she realized that Mr. B was right. If she controlled her movements, they still looked free and sweeping, but she also looked steadier and could go into the next movement easily.

Serenade was the first dance of the season on opening night, and Eva was proud to be a part of it. The dancers stood wearing blue dresses with long, tulle skirts, pink tights, and pink pointe shoes. With the same costume and their hair up in buns, it was hard to tell them apart. But when they danced in unison, it was a beautiful sight to behold. Eva felt like she was a part of a well-oiled machine that moved around the stage together perfectly, seventeen girls all moving as one. It was a thrill to be up there.

Later, her mother and Aunt Bea praised her dancing, and Ginny stared at her in awe. Now, also sixteen, Ginny was taller than Eva and had the figure of a woman. Eva was still petite and slender, looking younger than her years. But Ginny was impressed by her cousin.

"You were beautiful up there, twirling and swirling around in those lovely costumes," Ginny told her. "I envy your talent."

Eva smiled. "Thank you. I've worked hard to be up there."

"I know," Ginny said. "And it was worth all the work.

Someday, you'll be the star of the stage."

Eva's heart danced. She hoped that was true.

Mr. B approached Eva, carrying a bouquet of red roses. "For you, dear. You've worked hard, and you danced my ballets beautifully."

Eva was stunned as she accepted the roses. "You didn't have to do this," she said.

Mr. B laughed. "I didn't. I was given these by one of the patrons. But they belong to you for dancing beautifully." He nodded to Eva's mother, aunt, and cousin, then headed off to where the press was eager to ask him questions.

While Ginny and Bea watched in awe as Mr. B walked away, Gwen looked from the roses to her daughter.

"Be careful with him, dear," she whispered to Eva.

"He was just being kind," Eva told her mother. But when she went backstage to gather her things, the other dancers wouldn't look her in the eye. After having danced so beautifully together as one, now Eva felt like an outcast among them. Eva wasn't looking for any special attention from Mr. B, but the other girls seemed to think otherwise.

She left with her family for a late dinner, hoping the sick feeling in the pit of her stomach would pass. She had a whole season of dancing with the women who'd given her the cold shoulder backstage. She wouldn't be able to bear it if they all ignored her, just because of a dozen roses.

The next day, classes and rehearsals went on as usual, with no extra attention paid to her by Mr. B. Eva went about her work, ignoring lingering stares or whispering voices behind her back.

Because Eva had been so busy learning the dances, she'd had no time to check on her friend Mary. After rehearsals one evening, she took the bus to Mary's apartment building, where she lived with her parents. Eva had been there several times over the years, so she didn't think it would matter if she showed up uninvited.

Mary lived in a nicer apartment building than Eva's, which had a doorman and a concierge desk when she entered. The woman behind the desk asked who Eva was there to see, so she told her Mary Rasmussen. Once the woman hung up the phone, she asked Eva to take a seat, and Miss Rasmussen would be down shortly.

Eva was confused. Usually, she was told to go upstairs to the apartment. But she found a plush chair in the beautifully decorated lobby, sat, and waited.

Mary approached her a few minutes later.

"Oh, Mary! I'm so happy to see you," Eva said, springing up and hugging her. But Mary didn't make a move to hug Eva back, so she pulled away and looked at her friend. "Is everything okay?"

"Why are you here?" Mary asked, standing rigid and pushing her long, blond hair behind her shoulder.

"I came to see you," Eva said, stung by her sharp question. "I've been so busy, I haven't had a chance to run over to SAB and visit you."

Mary's face tightened. "So, you want to rub your success in my face?"

Eva's mouth dropped open. "No. Not at all. I've missed you."

"Then why has it taken you months to check on me?" Mary said. "I've been home all these months, and you haven't once dropped by."

"I was…I was busy," Eva said. "After I was asked to join the company, I had to learn new dances to be ready to tour upper New York, then I only had a month off in August."

"Oh, poor you." Mary crossed her arms. "Your dream came true, and you had no time for your friends."

Eva dropped her eyes. She felt hot tears form behind them. She'd thought Mary would be happy for her, but like the women in the company, she was jealous. "I'm sorry my being picked to dance upset you, but I can't help who is chosen and who isn't. You still have two years of classes and could be picked at any time. I was just lucky to be picked early."

"You really have been self-centered, haven't you?" Mary said. "You didn't even notice that I haven't returned to SAB for classes. I quit. There's no sense in my staying there if I'm never going to be a dancer."

"What?" Eva was stunned. "You quit? After all your years of training?"

Mary raised her chin. "I quit SAB, not ballet. I'm taking classes at the American Ballet Theater. They appreciate my talent there."

"Oh." Eva didn't know what to say. While she knew it was a good school, she would never have even thought of leaving SAB for ABT. Eva's dream had always been to dance for the NYCB, and Mr. B. "Well, I'm happy you're still dancing. I hope they see how talented you are and make you a member of the company soon."

"I have to go," Mary said, taking a step backward. "I have long days with school and dance, as you well know. Good luck with dancing for Mr. B."

"Thank you," Eva said. From Mary's tone, she could tell that she was being sarcastic. "Good luck to you, too," Eva told her.

With a heavy heart, Eva turned to leave the building. Was this how it would always be? She'd have no friends because of her accomplishments.

Suddenly, a hand tapped her shoulder, and she spun around. Mary was face-to-face with her, tears in her eyes. She hugged Eva close. "You danced beautifully in *Serenade*," Mary whispered in her ear. Then she let go and ran to the elevator.

Eva left, crying, and found her bus home.

* * *

Eva was busy all season, dancing in several different ballets each night and matinees on the weekends. She liked keeping busy. It made her forget that she had no time for friends and fun. Dancing was her entertainment, her livelihood, and her best friend.

"Dancing is everything," Mr. B told her when he saw her unhappy face one day after class. The other women never spoke to her, and he'd noticed that. "The better you get, the fewer friends you have. But dancing, you will always have that."

Eva nodded. She did love dancing, but sometimes she wished she had a friend she could share her feelings with. She rarely saw her mother, who was either working or out with Ray. And she rarely saw Ginny, who was busy with friends, school, and enjoying a normal teenage life. Eva's life was working, school, eating, sleeping—all in that order.

"Come with me," Mr. B said one afternoon after class, taking her hand and pulling her along with him. He led her to an empty studio, then waved in Randy, one of the young men in the company. Mr. B closed the door, stepped up to the record player, and began playing music.

"I want to work on something I've had on my mind a long time," Mr. B said. "It's a slow, but complicated piece, but I think it would be perfect for you two."

Mr. B. restarted the record and moved to the middle of the floor. When the melody began, Mr. B moved to the music, swaying this way and that, like a waltz, until the music grew faster and he spun and leaped around the room.

Eva watched, amazed at seeing Mr. B move so effortlessly across the floor. She'd seen him demonstrate many steps before, but never a full dance. It was mesmerizing to watch.

"There. Just like that," Mr. B said once he'd finished. He was breathing hard. "Did you get it all?" He laughed.

"I think you'll have to show me again," Eva said, laughing along.

"You will dance as partners," he said, moving Randy into position on the dance floor, then Eva. "Start together with the slow steps in unison, and then you will break away for the pirouettes and jumps. Then back together again and repeat. Let's try."

For over an hour, Mr. B showed Eva and Randy the steps, and they imitated him until Eva felt she'd memorized them. On the last try, she and Randy danced the short number with Mr. B on the sidelines, calling out his typical excited comments.

"Glide! Spin! Boom! Bang! Perfect!" he yelled as they spun, jumped, then swept across the floor.

"Ah, see? I told you that you two were perfect for this. We'll work more on it another day," Mr. B said. He left the room, leaving a stunned Eva and Randy behind.

"Did Mr. B just create a new dance on us?" Eva asked, hardly able to believe it was true. Mr. B only created dances for his lead dancers, whom he usually was in love with.

Randy looked equally surprised. "I think he just did." He smiled, and for the first time, Eva noticed how handsome he was. Randy was a little older than her but still new to the company. He'd come from the American Ballet Theater two years before and had been working hard to keep up with Balanchine's dance style.

They both left for their next rehearsal, but for the first time in months, Eva's heart felt light. It didn't matter if she had a good friend in the company. All that mattered was that she was dancing for George Balanchine and The New York City Ballet. That had to be enough.

Chapter Fifteen

Maddie

"Did you ever dance that new dance professionally?" Maddie asked when Eva finished telling her story.

Eva shook her head sadly. "No, I'm afraid not. I always wondered about it, but Mr. B never had us rehearse it again. But he brought Randy and me together, and we became good friends. And for that, I was thankful," Eva said.

"Maybe that was his intention all along," Sandy said. "It sounds like Mr. B was looking out for you."

Eva smiled. "I've thought that, too. He was only being kind to me, despite what the other women in the company thought. Another dancer soon became his favorite, but he didn't ignore me. He always had my interests at heart."

On the walk home, Maddie asked her mother if she was seriously considering teaching dance classes.

"Oh, I doubt it," Sandy said. "I barely have time for everything now. It's just a nice dream."

"But can't you make time for it?" Maddie asked. "If it's something you'd like to do, you should do it."

"I wish life were that easy," Sandy said. Then she shrugged. "I'll think about it, though."

That night after dinner, Maddie sat in her room writing down everything Eva had told her that day. It always amazed her that Eva knew exactly what she wanted her life to be from the time she was a child. Maddie knew she wanted to write for a living, but she wasn't sure how to go about it. Even if she went to school for creative writing, how would she support herself once she was out of college? It wasn't like a publisher would be waiting for her to write her first novel. But she also didn't want to spend years in college to work a minimum-wage job until—if ever—her big break came. It was all so discouraging.

After writing everything down, Maddie opened her laptop and typed in *Serenade* by George Balanchine. Dozens of videos popped up. Some were in black and white, others were newer in color. She scanned the dates but couldn't find any from the 1960s. So, she opened up a newer one and watched with the music turned up.

Maddie watched in awe. It was such a beautiful dance.

A knock came on her door, and her mother stuck her head inside. "What are you listening to?" Sandy asked.

"I'm watching a video of the ballet *Serenade*. The music is beautiful."

Sandy came in and sat on the bed beside her. A small smile played on her lips as she watched along with her daughter.

When the video was over, Maddie turned to her mother. "Eva danced this. Isn't that amazing? I wish there was a video from back then of her performance."

"I've danced a part of it, but only for a recital," Sandy said.

Maddie's brows rose. "Really? Eva taught it to you?"

"Yes. I danced the Russian Girl solo. It was so much fun.

The music was quick, and the steps were fast. I loved doing it."

Maddie watched her mother's face light up. Sandy was never this excited when she talked about her teaching job. "I can see how it would be fun." She waited a beat. "Are you sure you don't want to start dancing again?"

Sandy chuckled. "You're relentless."

"Sometimes," Maddie said. "When I feel it's important. Don't you think everyone should follow their dreams?"

Sandy turned serious. "Yes. I do. If it's possible." She moved her hand over Maddie's soft bedspread as if to smooth out invisible wrinkles. "And I hope it will be possible for you," she told Maddie. She smiled and left the room.

Chills ran up Maddie's spine. It was the first time her mother acknowledged she should follow her heart and not just be practical. Still, Maddie knew that being practical was the safe thing to do. But was it the right thing to do?

Maddie was busy the next week between working at the Freeze, mowing, and taking a two-day refresher course to prepare for the ACTs. She knew the course and the test cost money, and she wanted to do her best the first time and not have her parents waste money a second time on her. It was a lot of pressure, though. Cramming for a big test like that wasn't easy.

"I hate this," Livie said as they left the last day of class. "I know it will help us—maybe—but I feel like I just went through all my school years in two days."

"We did," Maddie said. "Honestly, I can't wait to get this test and the entire senior year over with. Everyone says that senior year is the best year of your life, but it's the most stressful. And it hasn't even started yet."

Livie and Maddie stopped at a small, local restaurant for

lunch. "I know how you feel, but I hate wishing my life away," Livie said. "Have you seen Caden lately? How's he doing?"

Maddie shrugged. "I don't know. I haven't seen him since I walked out on him last week. I hope he's getting better, but I don't think we can be a couple anymore. He doesn't take anything seriously. And I have to right now."

Livie nodded. "Aaron and I are kind of a thing right now. I hope that doesn't bother you."

"You are?" Maddie was surprised. "That's great. Caden always said that Aaron liked you. Sorry, I've been too self-absorbed lately to notice."

Livie smiled. "You've had a lot to deal with. We both have. My parents are pressuring me to go to the U of M next year, but I kind of like the idea of going to the University of Denver, where the other coach was from. It would be nice to get away from home—far away—where I can have a breather from my parents."

"Wow." Maddie was about to take a bite out of her burger, but set it back down. "Denver. That is far away. But I understand how you feel. There would be less pressure if you were farther away."

"Yeah." Livie toyed with her fries. "But my parents want to be able to attend my competitions, and they couldn't if I were that far away. So, who do I please? Me or my parents?"

Maddie shook her head. "I can't answer that. I have that same problem. Do I go to school for something practical to please my parents, or do the thing I want to do?"

"You could apply to DU, too," Livie said, her eyes brightening. "We could go together. I looked, and they have a really good creative writing program."

"That would be fun," Maddie said. She smiled. "Maybe I

will apply. Maybe we could share a dorm room."

Livie dropped Maddie off at her home, and she changed clothes to get ready for her shift at the Frosty Freeze. Ever since Carrie had become nicer, Maddie didn't mind working with her anymore. But she still preferred working with Livie.

Before leaving the house, Maddie's phone buzzed. She glanced at it and saw it was a text from Caden.

"So, are you ignoring me now?" he asked.

Maddie sighed. *"I've been really busy."*

"Aren't you going to come see me anymore? No one is visiting me here."

That didn't surprise Maddie. Livie had told her that Aaron got into a lot of trouble for attending the party, and the police kept pestering him for information. The last thing Aaron would want to do is hear Caden say it's not a big deal.

"I have to go to work. Take care," Maddie texted. She wanted to leave it at that. If they were breaking up, she didn't want to do it over the phone.

The Freeze was busy because it was so hot out, so everyone was grabbing an ice cream after being out on the lake all evening. Maddie tried to keep her mind on work, but Caden's text had bothered her. As long as she'd ignored him, she didn't worry about what was going on between them. But now, she had to face up to the fact that if she wanted to end it between them, she had to do it face-to-face. Maddie hated that idea.

"What's with you tonight?" Carrie asked as they cleaned up after yet another rush. "You're usually in a better mood."

"Boyfriend problems," Maddie said. She would have never discussed Caden with Carrie in the past, but now she felt like she could.

"What did he do now?" Carrie asked, rolling her eyes.

"Nothing. He's still in the hospital. But I've been ignoring him, hoping he'll go away," Maddie said. "I guess that isn't the mature way to end things."

Carrie's brows shot up. "You're going to end it with him? Wow. But I think it's a good idea. He was holding you back."

"I never thought that," Maddie said, defensively.

"Well, maybe he hasn't yet, but he will," Carrie said as she refilled the paper cups. "First, he'll beg you not to go away to college because he's not going, so you'll go to college here. Then, he'll distract you from your classes, and you'll start to flunk out. Before you know it, he'll be taking over your life while you still work here at the Freeze long after you two have five children."

Maddie was stunned. "Wow. You don't think too highly of me, do you? Do you really think I'd give up my future for a guy?"

Carrie stopped wiping the counter. "Sorry. I didn't mean to insult you. It's just that I've seen it a million times before with my friends from my hometown. And I almost got trapped that way, too. High school boyfriends are great if they want to continue to grow with you. But I get the feeling Caden is happy to stay a good-ole-boy and won't do much with his life."

"Well, you're right about that. He had no plans even before the accident." Maddie sighed. Deep down, she'd always known she and Caden weren't a good fit, but she'd always looked past that. And she did care about him. But now? It was finally time to move on.

The next day, after Maddie mowed a couple of lawns, she drew up all her courage and went to see Caden in the hospital. When she arrived, Aaron and Livie were in Caden's room. No one was talking, and the tension in the room was thick.

"Well, look who finally came to see me," Caden said, watching Maddie enter the room. "Did you all plan this? No one was here all last week."

"We didn't plan it," Aaron said through gritted teeth. "Why would we?"

"Maybe because you all feel guilty for abandoning me," Caden said. "I'm stuck here, and you all get to go on with your regular lives. It's not fair."

"Remember whose fault it is that you're here," Aaron said. He stood and reached for Livie's hand. "Let's go and let Maddie and Caden talk. See you later, Maddie."

"Bye," Maddie said as they left the room. She turned to Caden. "You shouldn't have been mean to them. You complained no one was coming to see you, and then you're rude."

Caden rolled his eyes. "None of you know what it's like to be stuck here in bed all day, every day. It sucks."

"I'm sure it does. But chasing everyone off doesn't help either," Maddie told him.

Caden frowned. "So, why are you here? Because I made you feel guilty?"

Maddie shook her head. "No. I came to talk."

"That can't be good," Caden said. "Are you really going to break up with me while I'm in the hospital? That's pretty low, Mads."

Maddie took a deep breath. "I think it's for the best. We've been arguing for a while now. We just aren't good for each other anymore. I'm sorry."

"We haven't been arguing—you've been arguing. All because of your stupid car!" Caden yelled. "I wish I'd never driven your dumb car. It's a piece of crap anyway."

Maddie stood. "Stop pushing your friends away, Caden. Pretty soon you won't have any."

"Hey, you're the one deserting me," Caden said. "So, go. You don't want to be here. Leave."

Maddie headed for the door. She turned in the doorway and looked at Caden. "I had hoped we could at least be friends. I'm not angry with you. It's just that we both want different things out of life."

"Friends? Right!" Caden's face turned red with anger. "I don't want you as a friend. You were my girlfriend, not a *friend*. Just go. I don't need you. I don't need Aaron either. I have plenty of *friends!*"

Maddie sighed. "I hope you get better soon," she said softly. "Goodbye." She walked down the hallway and to the elevator. Her heart was racing, but she was surprised that she didn't feel sad. She felt relieved. Breaking up with Caden was the right thing to do.

* * *

Maddie was busy all week mowing lawns and working. She almost had enough to pay back her parents for the car repairs. Her car had been fixed, but was still at the shop waiting until Maddie paid her parents back.

The funny thing was that Maddie didn't resent her parents for making her wait to drive her car. She'd been working so hard all summer to earn money, and she actually felt good that she would be able to pay them back. She was proud of herself.

Coming home one afternoon, Maddie noticed that the Jeep was in the driveway, but when she walked inside, her sister was sitting at the counter, eating lunch alone.

"Where's Mom?" Maddie asked. She went to the fridge to see what she could make herself for lunch.

"She left to go on a run a few minutes ago," Lily said, taking a bite out of her sandwich.

"In this heat? She always runs in the morning when it's cool."

"She's been running later this past week," Lily said. "It's weird, though. She had on a loose sweater and leggings when she left today. That's a lot to wear running in this heat."

Maddie frowned. That was weird.

She found some leftovers from the previous night and heated them for lunch, then sat down at the counter with Lily. "How's gymnastics?" Maddie asked.

Lily shrugged. "Okay. I have a competition in Duluth next week. Are you coming?"

"I'll try," Maddie said, then asked her for the details. It would be fun to see her sister compete.

Sandy walked through the kitchen door just as Maddie was cleaning up the lunch dishes.

"How was your run?" Maddie asked.

"Run?" Sandy stared at her for a moment. "Oh, yeah. It was fine."

"Weren't you hot in all those clothes?" Maddie asked. "It's almost ninety out there."

"Huh?" Sandy pulled a water bottle from the fridge. "Oh. No. I was fine." She called out to Lily, who was in the living room watching a game show. "I'm going to rinse off, and then I'll take you to gymnastics."

"Okay," Lily mumbled, barely listening.

Maddie watched her mother go up the stairs. Something was off, but she couldn't quite figure out what.

"I'm going over to Eva's house to check on their lawn," Maddie told Lily. "See you later."

Once again, Lily mumbled, barely paying attention to her.

Maddie walked slowly down the road toward Eva and Ginny's house. She thought about how weird her mother was acting. Maybe it was just the heat. These hot days made everyone a little edgy.

When she arrived at the big house, she saw that they didn't need it mowed yet. The heat, along with the lack of rain, had pretty much dried up the grass. Still, Maddie walked up the steps to the house to check in and let them know she was keeping an eye on the lawn.

"Oh, lovely," Eva said when she answered the door. "You're here! Come inside."

"I didn't want to bother you. I just wanted you to know that I'm watching the lawn," Maddie said.

"Watching it do what?" Ginny piped up. "It's dying out there in this heat."

Maddie laughed. "It is. But these heat spells always end with a big thunderstorm, so we'll have rain soon."

"Come in anyway, and I can tell you more of my story," Eva said. "Let's sit on the sofa today. It's more comfortable."

"Are you hungry?" Ginny asked. "We already had lunch."

"I ate lunch before I came," Maddie said.

"But we can always have a few of Ginny's gingersnaps," Eva said. "And some iced tea."

"Oh, that sounds good," Maddie said. Ginny baked the best gingersnap cookies.

"I suppose you want me to go get some, then," Ginny complained.

Maddie and Eva laughed. They both knew that Ginny was

happy to bring them out.

"Did you write down what I told you the last time?" Eva asked, her blue eyes twinkling.

"I did. It still amazes me how much you accomplished by age sixteen," Maddie told her. "I'm a year older than that, and I've accomplished nothing."

"Oh, dear," Eva said. "Don't say that. You have your whole life ahead of you to accomplish great things. Being a ballerina, you only have a few good years in your youth to shine. You have to start early. I was one of the lucky ones to start at sixteen. Most joined the company at eighteen."

"Well, I'm still impressed," Maddie said.

Ginny brought a plate of cookies and three glasses of iced tea on a tray. She set it on the coffee table, then sat in the brown leather chair. "There. We're all set for story time."

Chuckling, Eva began talking. "I was in the corps de ballet for two years, and then Mr. B moved me up to soloist. That was so exciting. Soloists dance important roles in many of the ballets. It's not as incredible as being a principal dancer, but it's close. The soloists have a bigger dressing room that they share, and we didn't dance as many roles as we did in the corps, but when we did dance, everyone's eyes were on us. In many of my parts, I was partnered with Randy, which was fun. He and I were good friends and enjoyed rehearsing together. Then, after two years dancing as a soloist, something exciting happened. We were asked to go on a tour to dance in the Soviet Union and in Europe. I can't tell you how incredibly excited, yet terrified, we all were."

CHAPTER SIXTEEN

Eva - 1962

Eva was excited. The NYCB was going away for three months to dance in the Soviet Union and Europe. She could hardly believe it.

During her years dancing with the company, Eva had traveled around the United States to perform, but never out of the country. And now, they were going on the trip of a lifetime.

Although the trip almost didn't happen. Mr. Balanchine did not want to go to the Soviet Union. After growing up in St. Petersburg—he attended the Imperial Theater School to learn to dance, despite his real love being music—during the revolution, when Czar Nicholas II was forced to abdicate, Mr. B never wanted to see the Soviet Union again. He remembered death, starvation, and tyranny, and after enjoying freedom in the United States, he didn't wish to revisit his terrible childhood.

Mr. B was also afraid. He'd come to the U.S. with questionable papers Lincoln Kirstein had obtained for him, and he didn't want to be forced to stay in Russia.

But the U.S. State Department talked him into going

as a goodwill gesture. The two countries were deep into the Cold War, and sending the NYCB and Balanchine to dance in Russia, while Russia's Bolshoi Ballet toured the U.S. and Canada, was meant to help bring the two countries closer.

So, Mr. B relented.

After summer break, the dancers worked in earnest on rehearsals for their tour. Mr. B, normally quite calm and collected, seemed almost frenzied during those rehearsals. He wanted his dancers to be perfect. His ballets were going to be seen around the world, and he meant to make his adoptive country proud of him.

"More! More!" Mr. B shouted as he watched a young male dancer jump into the air. "Higher! Faster!"

"Don't think! Just do!" he told another dancer as she stumbled over some difficult steps. "Dance from the heart! Feel it in your soul!"

When it was Eva's turn to practice a short solo for the tour, her nerves were on edge. She feared Mr. B's disapproval of her dancing and sending her back into the corps. As she spun in a fast pirouette with her partner close by to help her balance at the end, there was only silence. Once she'd completed her steps, Mr. B shook his head.

"Dear. It was good but not great. What are you saving it for? Give your all now, not later."

Eva was embarrassed at first, until his words hit her and she understood. Every rehearsal, every dance, Mr. B expected his dancers to give one hundred and ten percent of themselves. So, when she spun the second time, she used all her strength and gave it her all.

"Brava!" Mr. B yelled. "That is how it is done!"

Eva walked away from the rehearsal feeling relieved and

encouraged by Mr. B's praise.

Eva was still struggling with another significant change in her life right before they left on the tour. Her mother and her long-time gentleman friend, Ray, had married six months prior and moved to northern Minnesota. Ray was close to retirement age and wanted to return to a slower way of life. He owned a nice cabin on Cedar Lake that he wanted to remodel and make larger for them to live in. After sharing an apartment with her mother for twenty years, Eva felt lost without her around. Eva had kept their apartment because she could afford the rent on her salary, but it was strange not having her mother there anymore.

In August, sixty-one dancers, along with Mr. B, Lincoln Kirstein, Betty Cage, the company doctor, and four conductors and four pianists gathered at Idlewild Airport in New York for the first leg of their three-month journey. The stage manager and a small crew went along, too, as did the wardrobe personnel. Mothers of three of the underage dancers went, too, to act as chaperones.

Eva, now age twenty, wished her mother could come along, too, but she was starting her new life in Minnesota with her husband, so Eva didn't ask her. So, along with the other dancers, Eva traveled alone for the first time.

Mr. B was wonderful, checking on everyone to make sure no one was left behind. Their first month would be spent in Europe, then they would spend two months touring the Soviet Union. The safety of his dancers was Mr. B's number one priority.

"Stay together and don't wander around alone in the cities we visit," Mr. B told everyone. "Especially in the Soviet Union. We don't want them to find an excuse to arrest any of you."

Eva took his warnings seriously. As much as she wanted to explore all the places they visited, she also realized he was right. She hoped some of them could Europe as a group if they were careful.

Over the past two years, Mr. B had found a new favorite dancer. While Eva was still given good solo roles to dance, she was happy that Mr. B no longer paid a lot of attention to her. The new dancer was a young woman, so of course, many of the older dancers were jealous and spoke badly of her. But Eva liked her and didn't mind that she was his favorite. And now, the other dancers had accepted Eva into their circle of friendship, so she finally had friends again.

"It's all silly," Randy said quietly to Eva on the flight to Amsterdam. "The women in the company can be so petty."

Eva laughed. "Oh, and you men never get jealous over roles you wish you'd been chosen for. If I remember right, you had hoped to be a principal dancer by now, like Jacques."

Randy shrugged. "Okay. You're right. But at least I get to dance with you most of the time. We make a good pair."

"We do." Eva loved dancing with Randy and was always happy when Mr. B paired them. He was the right height for her, even when she was on pointe, and they had danced together for so long now that they knew each other's strengths and weaknesses. When she jumped into his arms, she knew he'd always catch her. That meant a lot when you were putting your fate into someone else's arms.

They didn't dance in Amsterdam, but began their tour in Hamburg, Germany. Audiences loved them, but unfortunately, luck was not on their side. Principal dancer, Jacques d'Amboise, and soloist, Victoria Simon, were hit by a trolley car and sustained injuries. With broken ribs and a concussion, Jacques was unable to dance his lead role in *Apollo* and other ballets, so the company was immediately put into a tailspin. Conrad Ludlow was moved into Jacques's role, but that meant repositioning others in the dances. Eva was given an additional solo to allow another female soloist to move into Victoria's spot. While that was good for Eva's career, it upset many to see her being given a prime role instead of them.

"Good for you, not for me," Randy complained one day during dance class. They still had classes to stay limber and in shape for each night's performance.

"Gee, thanks," Eva said. "I can't control who they give dances to."

"Sorry," Randy said, looking sheepish. "I had hoped to dance the lead in *Apollo*. I should have known they'd never give it to lowly old me."

"Your day will come," Eva told him. She felt bad for him, but she wasn't a principal dancer either. It wasn't like any of them had a say in what ballets they danced.

They traveled through Europe with excellent reviews, all the time having to switch up dancers because of someone's hurt knee or twisted ankle. Eva was given different solos she'd never rehearsed before and had to learn them quickly.

"That is why I give them to you," Mr. B told her one afternoon while she worked at learning a new solo. "You pick up the steps easily."

While Eva appreciated his compliment, she knew she didn't pick steps up easily. It took time and work to learn a new solo in just a few hours. Randy helped her at times, and so did Jacques, who had healed by then. But it was still difficult.

Finally, the day came when they arrived in the Soviet Union. As they departed their plane in Moscow, Mr. B had all the dancers go out before him. Then, he came down the stairs with his principal dancer, Diane Adams, on his arm as the press, Soviet officials, and American diplomats all greeted him.

"Welcome to Russia, home of classical ballet," a diplomat said to Balanchine as the press watched and taped his return to Russia. But Mr. B would not let it stand at that.

"No, Russia is the home of Romantic ballet," Mr. B said, his head held high. "America is the home of classical ballet."

Eva and the other dancers held their breath, waiting for an angry reply from the diplomat, but none came. Balanchine had made his point. He was proud to have created a new style of ballet and would not allow his former country to take credit for it.

Soon, Mr. B's younger brother, Andrei, whom he hadn't seen in nearly forty years—not since the day Balanchine had been left at the Imperial Theater School at only nine years old—approached him and they hugged in greeting. It was a heartwarming scene, and Eva even had tears in her eyes.

The dance company was placed at the Hotel Ukraine, which, compared to their prior hotels in Europe, was sparsely furnished and cold. The dancers were warned not to say anything political or negative about the Soviet Union, even in their rooms, because listening devices were everywhere. When Eva finally obtained her room key from the sullen-looking floor matron that first night, she was shocked at how horrible the room was. There were only two small camp beds, a dresser, and a tiny bathroom. She was sharing the room with another soloist, and both women held their tongues so as not to say anything that might get them into trouble. But from the look on each other's faces, they knew what the other was thinking.

But all the dancers were professionals, and they were there

to do one thing—dance. And to make the NYCB and George Balanchine look good. So, that is what they did, night after night, to audiences that held back their enthusiasm, yet continued to pack in both the Bolshoi Theater and the Palace of Congresses.

Eva went along with a few other dancers during the day to tour the city, but they were always aware of being watched. The women had been told to wear dresses only because they were representing the United States. The gay men in the company were also warned to be discreet. One wrong move and they'd be thrown in jail. It was a unique, if somewhat scary, situation for them all.

The food situation wasn't much better. They all ate in a large dining room downstairs at their hotel, and there weren't many food choices. Very few vegetables were available, and potatoes, bread, and white sauce were often served. Eva was thankful they'd been warned about the scarcity of good food, and each dancer had brought along a trunk of food to hold them over until they returned home.

One thing the dancers were not told was that while they were entertaining the people of Russia, the Cuban Missile Crisis was happening between the United States, Russia, and Cuba. Later, Eva learned that the American Embassy in the Soviet Union had told Lincoln Kirstein and Betty Cage that if problems arose from the crisis, the embassy would not be able to help them.

That night, the dancers took their places and danced as usual, most unaware of what might happen. After they danced, the crowd cheered for more. But Mr. B took the stage, thanked them, then told the crowd that the dancers would be back the next day.

Luckily, the crisis was averted, and the dancers did perform the next day. As rumors spread throughout the company, they soon learned of the tragedy that could have occurred had the two countries gone to war. Thankfully, they did not.

As they danced through the Soviet Union, the dancers grew weary from fatigue and the lack of healthy food, and from the constant stress of being watched. The day they flew out of the Soviet Union, their spirits rose. They were going home.

As soon as they arrived in New York City, one of the NYCB patrons gave a reception in her home for Mr. Balanchine, Lincoln Kirstein, and the principal and soloist dancers in the company. Mr. B complained about having to attend the black-tie affair, but Eva was excited. She'd never gone to such a fancy reception before. It felt like such a grown-up thing to do.

Eva asked Ginny to help her find a cocktail dress suitable for the event. Since her funds were low, they crossed the Brooklyn Bridge and went to the well-known Loehmann's Department store to shop.

Eva found a simple black chiffon dress with a V-front and back and a full, flowing skirt. She bought patent-leather black kitten-heel shoes to wear with it. It was a simple, but elegant dress that suited her young age.

"I love it!" Ginny said when Eva tried it on. "So chic yet simple. I wish I had somewhere fancy to go. All my friends do is go to the movies or drink coffee in the local café." Ginny had attended business college for two years after high school and now worked as a secretary in an insurance office.

"Doesn't your boyfriend, Marty, take you anywhere fancy?" Eva asked as she turned this way and that in front of the mirror, admiring the dress. Ginny and Marty had been dating for six months.

Ginny shrugged. "He used to take me dancing or out for a nice meal, but lately, we just watch television at my parents' house or grab dinner at a cheap restaurant. I know he's saving to get his own apartment, but it would be fun to go out somewhere nice."

"This is the first time I've been anywhere fancy," Eva said. "And at least you have a boyfriend. I've never dated anyone before. I'm too busy dancing."

"What about that Randy guy you dance with? Doesn't he have a thing for you?" Ginny asked.

Eva laughed. "We're just friends and dance partners. He thinks of me as a sister. When we were on tour, he walked with me to places and watched over me, but he has no real designs on me."

"Do you want him to?" Ginny asked, her brows raised suggestively.

"No, not really. But it would be fun to have a boyfriend," Eva said. "Mr. B says we should only have boyfriends and never get married. He thinks that dancers who marry become Mrs. So-and-So and lose their identity as a dancer."

Ginny frowned. "Isn't Mr. Balanchine married? To a former dancer?"

"Yes, he is. But that's different." Eva laughed. "Mr. B is full of advice. He just doesn't want to lose his best dancers."

The next night, Eva, escorted by Randy, accompanied the other dancers and Mr. B, who escorted his latest favorite dancer to come along with him, to a high-rise apartment building in Manhattan. The elevator took them up to the penthouse, and when they walked in, Eva gasped. The place was large and beautiful, with gorgeous furniture and breathtaking views of the city.

"It's nice to have money, no?" Mr. B whispered to her with a grin.

Eva agreed. She'd never seen an apartment so spacious and lavishly furnished. There was a crowd of people there, anxious to meet Mr. B and the dancers who toured the Soviet Union. Everyone was stylishly dressed, drinking wine, champagne, and cocktails. Waiters and waitresses walked through the crowd, offering a variety of delicious appetizers.

"Do you want a drink?" Randy asked her as a waiter with a tray of champagne glasses walked by.

"I've never had champagne or any alcohol before," Eva said, feeling childish. She was twenty years old and had very little life experience.

"We'll ignore the fact that you are underage and let you try some tonight," Randy said with a grin. He lifted two champagne flutes from the tray and handed one to Eva.

Tentatively, she sipped the bubbly liquid. Her face flushed as the drink went down. "It's good," she told Randy.

"And it's free," he whispered. "So, enjoy. But first we should eat something so you don't get drunk."

Randy was much more socially adept at meeting new people than Eva, so she stayed near him as they spoke to the many people in the room. The women wanted to know how it felt to dance so beautifully on stage, and the men wanted to know if she was single. The women also took a great interest in Randy, gushing over his dancing and good looks. Eva couldn't help but smile. Randy loved attention, but the women dripping in diamonds and emeralds were practically drooling over him.

"Your boyfriend seems to have attracted a lot of attention," a man with dark, wavy hair and a British accent said to Eva as the older women pushed her aside. With two glasses of champagne in her, she was no longer shy.

"He loves attention," she said. "And he's not my boyfriend. He's my dance partner."

The handsome young man's cool blue eyes lit up as he smiled at her. "That's good to hear. Can I get you a fresh glass?" He nodded to the champagne flute in her hand.

"Thank you, but I'd better not. It's already going to my head," Eva told him. She looked him up and down, trying not to be obvious. He was quite handsome in his tuxedo.

"I'm Colin," the man said, offering his hand. "Colin Hughes."

Eva placed her hand in his to shake, but instead, he lifted hers to his lips and placed a soft kiss on it. It was so unexpected, Eva's heart pounded in her chest. She'd never had a man do such a thing before.

"I'm Eva Ashford," she told him, breathlessly. "It's nice to meet you."

Colin smiled again, his eyes twinkling, as he still held her hand. "My dear. It is most definitely nice to meet you."

Eva's face heated in a blush, and she gently retrieved her hand. Feeling nervous, she spoke quickly. "Are you friends with the hostess?"

Colin reached for a glass of white wine as a server passed by, but continued to smile at Eva. "It's really my father who's a friend of the hostess. But the ladies about town always invite me to their parties. I think they're all conniving to marry me off to one of their daughters."

"Well, then. You must be careful," Eva said playfully. "You'd hate to be married off to some spoiled rich girl."

Colin stared at her for a moment, then laughed out loud. The people around them stopped and stared, then went back to their own chatter.

"I think you are quite right," Colin said. "How lucky I am that you're here to save me from that fate."

They found a quiet corner of the room by a large window overlooking New York City and sat in soft, comfortable chairs. As they talked, the rest of the guests faded away, and Eva felt like they were the only two people in the room. Colin spoke of his childhood in an English boarding school and traveling all over the world with his father, who owned real estate everywhere.

"My mothers—yes, plural—came and went as my father remarried often, but my father was usually around and attentive. So, I guess I'm lucky about that," Colin said, sipping his wine. They had taken an entire tray of hors d'oeuvres from a waiter and were enjoying them.

"What happened to your real mother?" Eva asked, intrigued. "Did you see her much?"

Colin shook his head. "She was a young socialite when she married my father, and once I was born, she couldn't sit still. So, she came back to New York City and found a new husband, and I never see her."

"I'm sorry," Eva said. "Although I do understand how it feels to have only one parent. My father left us when I was young, and I don't know him at all. But my mother was my constant companion all through my childhood. Only recently did she remarry and move away, but I'm happy for her."

"Well then, we can both be partial orphans together," Colin said, his eyes twinkling when he smiled.

The time went by quickly, and soon Mr. B approached the young couple in the corner.

"Eva, dear. We are all leaving now," he said, studying Colin with sharp eyes. He offered his arm to her as she stood, and she placed her arm through his.

"It was nice talking with you," Eva told Colin, who'd politely stood to say goodbye.

"I hope to see you again soon," Colin said, giving her a small bow. He nodded his head to Mr. B before Eva, and Balanchine turned and headed for the door.

"Watch out for that one, dear," Mr. B whispered in her ear. "He's a bit too sleek."

Eva frowned. "Sleek?"

"No, dear. Sleek. Like oil through your fingers. Slippery," Mr. B said in his thick accent.

Eva wanted to laugh, but she knew Mr. B was being serious. "Oh, you mean slick. Don't worry, I'll be careful," she said. "But he seems harmless."

As they approached the group of dancers waiting at the front door, Mr. B shook his head. "No man is harmless around a sweet young lady like you." He helped her on with her coat, and they all made their way to the elevator.

Eva didn't care what Mr. B thought about Colin. She'd given him her phone number—the first man she'd ever done that with—and she hoped he would call her.

Chapter Seventeen

Maddie

Maddie thought about Eva's story and how Mr. B called the man she'd met slick. While it was a funny story, it also made her think of her now ex-boyfriend, Caden. She would describe him as slick. He'd drawn her in almost a year ago by being extraordinarily nice to her, and then it slowly fell apart as his real personality shone through. Too bad Maddie hadn't had a Mr. B to warn her.

Although she had to admit, her father had often mentioned his dislike for Caden, and Maddie hadn't listened. So, maybe she would have ignored Mr. B's advice, too.

Maddie had already written down the most recent story Eva had told her, and she was excited to hear more. If she didn't have to mow so many lawns and work at the Freeze, she'd be over there every day listening to Eva talk.

Maddie spent another week mowing a few lawns, despite the heat, and took some time to hang out by the lake with Lily and Livie. Even though her sister and best friend were five years apart in age and at different levels in gymnastics, they had a lot in common. So, as they lay on a towel on the beach near the water, Livie and Lily compared accomplishments, competitions won and lost, and goals for their future in the sport.

"I hope I get a scholarship to college for gymnastics like you've been offered," Lily told Livie. I want to compete professionally, and college is the best place to start."

"Wow. You're already planning that?" Maddie said. "You aren't even in high school yet."

"So," Lily said defensively. "I know that's what I want to do. I have a lot of time to work toward it."

"You know more than I did at your age," Livie said. "I love gymnastics, but I never saw it as a way to have my college paid for. Although it is a good way to save my parents' money."

"But do you love it enough to compete for the next few years?" Maddie asked.

"I guess I do," Livie said. "It's easier to be seen if you're on a college team than just attending competitions to try to make the Olympic Team. That's always been my goal."

"That would be amazing," Lily said. "My coach says that because we come from such a small town, we probably won't ever make it that far."

Aghast, Livie lifted herself on her elbows and looked over at Lily. "How can she say such a thing? Is that the new coach? Well, don't believe her. Just because she never went far with gymnastics doesn't mean you won't."

Maddie smiled at how determined Livie sounded. She loved that Livie cared enough about her little sister to tell her she had no limits to her dreams.

When Maddie and Lily arrived home, their mother was just coming in, too.

"Where did you go?" Maddie asked, noticing she was

wearing leggings and a loose sweater over a tank top again.

Sandy frowned at her. "Am I supposed to tell you everything I do?"

Taken aback, Maddie said, "Sorry. I was just asking."

Sandy sighed. "I was out for a run, that's all. Did you girls have fun at the beach?"

Maddie stared at her mother's clothes. She never wore a big sweater when she went running, especially when it was in the eighties outside. "Yeah. Did you know Lily has plans to get a gymnastics scholarship for college? She's planning out her life early."

Sandy poured a glass of ice water and took a long drink. "I think it's great that she's so focused."

"It's a lot of pressure on a twelve-year-old," Maddie said.

Sandy shrugged. "Life is a lot of pressure. At least she knows what she wants. And besides, she could wake up tomorrow and hate gymnastics, so you never know what life will bring."

Maddie was shocked at how pessimistic her mom sounded. Her mother was usually the optimistic one.

That evening, Maddie worked a shift with Carrie at the Freeze. They had their usual late afternoon rush, then things quieted down.

"What are you studying at college?" Maddie asked Carrie. "I don't think you've ever mentioned your major."

"Business Management with a minor in Accounting," Carrie said. She grinned. "Sounds exciting, doesn't it?"

Maddie laughed as she wiped down the ice cream machines. "Is that what you were always interested in?"

"Oh, yeah. Right," Carrie said. "As a child, I was always playing office manager and doing my parents' taxes."

"Okay," Maddie said. "I realize it's something you decided

to do at some point. When you were a child, what did you want to be when you grew up?"

Carrie studied Maddie for a moment. "Don't laugh. I wanted to be a ballerina."

"Really?" Maddie was stunned. "Did you take dance lessons as a little girl?"

"Of course," Carrie said. "I started ballet when I was five and did it until I was fifteen."

"Why did you stop?" Maddie asked.

Carrie shrugged. "Boys. Friends. I didn't want to spend my evenings doing pliés and relevés when I could be at the movies or hanging out at the mall with my friends."

"Are you sorry you quit?" Maddie asked.

Carrie's eyes narrowed. "What is this, twenty questions?"

Maddie laughed. "No. My little sister told me today she has her life all planned out already at age twelve. I'm just wondering if I'm the only one who doesn't have her life planned out."

Carrie shook her head. "No. Everyone is messed up, not just you. I've changed my major twice already. First, I was going to be a grade-school teacher, but after my first year working in this place, I decided I wasn't a fan of sticky-fingered kids." Carrie laughed. "So, I changed to Business. As you can guess, I'm a stickler for rules and numbers, so it suits me."

"Well, you do like to do things by the book," Maddie said, grinning.

"Don't worry about twenty years from now," Carrie said. "Pick a college, go, and you'll find a major you like eventually. None of us has everything figured out."

Maddie nodded as she continued to work, cleaning the place. Her mother had basically said the same thing.

A thunderstorm hit late that night, and the weather turned

cooler. It was a relief to have lower humidity and cooler temps. It was already the first week of August, so they still had many more hot days to look forward to.

Halfway through the week, Maddie walked down to Eva and Ginny's house to check on their lawn and gardens. Even if she didn't have to mow, she could hear more of Eva's story. She climbed the stone steps and knocked on the orange door. Now that she knew the ladies, Maddie smiled every time she saw the brightly painted door.

From inside, she heard a piano playing. Was Ginny playing? She always complained she couldn't play piano anymore because of her arthritis. When no one answered her knock, she walked along the wooden path through the garden over to the French doors connected to the large room. Peering inside, Maddie saw Ginny sitting at the piano across the room, and Eva was sitting in a chair, tapping her cane to the music. It warmed her heart to see the ladies enjoying themselves.

Suddenly, another figure came into view. A woman walked to one of the ballet barres, placed one hand on it, and began to move. Her movements were graceful and smooth as she performed deep pliés, while her arm moved in unison. Was Eva teaching again?

Spellbound, Maddie watched as the woman moved, then turned to the other side and followed along with the music again. Her brown hair was in a ponytail, and she wore black leggings, a tank top, and ballet slippers. Realization hit Maddie, and she stepped back from the door and gasped. The graceful woman was her mother!

The music stopped, and a face appeared in the window, staring at Maddie. Maddie jumped.

"Well, are you going to stand there staring or are you

coming in?" Ginny called through the door. "The front door is unlocked."

Embarrassed at being caught, but curious about what was happening, Maddie moved to the front door and stepped inside. She walked through the open doors of the great room, and there stood Ginny, Sandy, and Eva.

"What's going on?" Maddie asked when no one said a word.

Eva smiled. "Come in, dear. We're having dance class."

Maddie walked closer to Eva and noticed her mother looked as embarrassed as she felt. She suddenly felt bad for intruding on her mother's secret dance lesson. "I'm sorry," Maddie said. "I came to check on the lawn and gardens, and I heard music. I can leave if you want me to."

Her mother was still across the room, and she quickly pulled on her big sweater and picked up her sneakers. "I was finished anyway," she said.

"There's no need to stop yet," Eva said, looking disappointed. "You were just warming up."

"I should probably get Lily to gymnastics," Sandy said.

Maddie felt terrible. "Don't leave, Mom. Lily is happily watching a game show on TV and eating lunch. She's fine. I can go."

"Neither of you is leaving," Ginny said, taking charge of the situation. "I'm making lunch for all of us." Ginny turned toward the kitchen and walked away.

"That will be lovely," Eva said cheerfully as if everything were fine. "Maddie, dear. Come help me set the table." Eva stood and walked slowly to the small dining room. Maddie had no choice but to follow.

Sandy followed, too. Maddie busied herself getting napkins and silverware and placing them on the table while Eva sat down on one of the chairs.

"Your mother is still in wonderful dancing shape," Eva said, sounding proud. "As I'd told her, you never forget how to move."

Maddie finally looked directly at her mother, and their eyes met. "Is this where you've been instead of running?"

Sandy nodded. "Yes. Eva has been kind enough to let me practice so I could decide if I wanted to teach dancing."

"I've been playing the piano," Ginny piped up from the kitchen. "That's no small thing."

The others smiled.

"You've been wonderful," Sandy told Ginny. "You haven't lost your touch."

Ginny turned and looked at Sandy. "And neither have you. You should have been dancing all these years, but better late than never."

"Are you going to start teaching dance?" Maddie asked.

"I'm thinking seriously about it," Sandy said. She winced. "Do you think it's crazy of me to do this after all these years?"

Maddie had never seen her mother so unsure of herself. Maybe being an adult didn't mean you had everything figured out. "No. I think if you want to do this, you should."

Sandy sighed. "I didn't realize how much I'd missed ballet. Working out here with Eva has reminded me what a big part of my life it was for all those years. And how wonderful it feels to dance."

"Life's too short not to do what you love," Ginny said, bringing over plates of salad with cold grilled chicken on the side. "Look at us. Our lives have sped by so quickly. You have to make time for what you want to do."

"Well said, Ginny," Eva said. "I almost lost dance once,

too, but I would have lost a piece of my soul if I hadn't been able to teach it." She reached over and patted Sandy's hand. "You know you're welcome to use our studio for classes any time you want. It would be refreshing to have this place come back to life again."

"You're much too kind, Eva," Sandy said. "I'll think it over. There's a lot to consider between my family and work."

"Find a way, dear. It will fill up your soul." Eva smiled at her and winked.

Later that evening, as the family sat around the dinner table, Sandy hesitantly brought up the subject of teaching ballet. "I could teach classes two nights a week during the school year and then three or four days a week in the summer," she said.

"Wait, what?" This was the first her husband had heard of it. "When did you start dancing again? Hasn't it been years?"

"Mom has been practicing at Eva and Ginny's house," Maddie said, excited that her mother was seriously considering it. She's really good."

"Well, I'm not fully there yet, but I can practice the rest of the summer," Sandy said. "I'd mostly be teaching the basics to young girls and boys, not seasoned dancers."

"But Mom," Maddie said. "You were trained for years by a woman who danced for George Balanchine. Think about it. You'll be passing down the Balanchine method of ballet. That's a big legacy."

Matt stared from Sandy to Maddie, looking totally confused. "What about your teaching job? You're not going to quit it, are you?"

"No, of course not," Sandy said. "But I can do this, too. It won't be easy, but it's something I love. And it will bring in extra money."

Lily was frowning. "You mean the past couple of weeks when you said you were running, you were really at the witches' house dancing?"

"They're not witches!" Maddie and Sandy said in unison, then laughed.

"They're nice older ladies," Maddie said. "You really should come with me and meet them," she told Lily.

"I'm confused," Lily said.

"Well, that makes two of us," Matt said. "But hey, if you want to work another job, be my guest. With Maddie going to college, we could use an extra income."

Sandy shook her head and set down her silverware. "You don't understand, Matt. It's more than just a job. It's something I've been missing for years. Decades! It's something I love to do, and I can teach others at the same time."

"Whatever you want to do, hon, I'm behind you," Matt said gently. "I hadn't realized you'd missed dancing so much."

"Me, either. Seeing Eva again and the studio just brought it all back to me. I really want to do this."

Lily studied her mom for a moment. "You should do it, Mom. I love gymnastics, and I get to do that. And dad plays golf all summer because he loves it. You should do what you love, too."

Sandy smiled at her youngest daughter. "Thanks, sweetie. You're right." She turned to Maddie. "We should all do what we love."

A chill ran up Maddie's spine. She knew in that moment, her mother was giving her permission to forget about being practical and to follow her dream.

Chapter Eighteen

Eva – 1962

Now that the ballet company was back from their tour, they immediately began rehearsing for the Christmas season. It was time again for the holiday favorite, *The Nutcracker,* and everyone was excited to be performing this beautiful ballet once again. Much to Eva's surprise, she was given a new role in the ballet.

"Mr. B would like you to learn the role of Dewdrop in the Waltz of the Flowers this year," the ballet mistress told Eva one day after class. "You'll have to learn it quickly. This will be in addition to you dancing in the Waltz of the Snowflakes."

Eva was stunned but pleased. Dewdrop was a lead role. While they often chose a principal dancer for that part, they sometimes chose a soloist, and this was her chance to show Mr. B her skills.

She also knew she would be working twice as hard as the year before, dancing in two separate Acts. But since the snowflake dance was in Act I, and the flower dance was in Act II, it gave her plenty of time to change costumes and return to the stage.

The principal dancer who'd danced Dewdrop the year before rehearsed with Eva so she could learn the part. The steps were not easy. The dance consisted of quick steps, several series of pirouettes, and jumps. It was a demanding role, but she was excited to dance it.

"You know I chose you because of your perfect jumps," Mr. B told her one day after watching rehearsal. "Make sure you leap with all your strength and energy. Like a cat!" He motioned with his arm the way a cat leaps from one spot to another, then chuckled.

"I won't hold back. I'll do it like it's the only time I'll ever dance," Eva told him. "Like you always tell us."

"Good girl. I knew you were perfect for the part."

Since *The Nutcracker* was the only ballet the NYCB performed over the holidays, Eva had only those two parts to practice, which made her schedule lighter. But they also performed at least twice a day. When she received a call from Colin, she accepted his invitation to lunch since dinner was out of the question because she'd be dancing most evenings.

"You are a difficult lady to get in contact with," Colin teased her when they finally met at a small but charming restaurant in downtown Manhattan. Colin had offered to pick her up, but she'd had class that morning and had to rush to make it to lunch.

"Sorry," Eva said contritely. "I'm never home. I'm in class in the morning and have rehearsals in the afternoon. I actually had to skip a practice this afternoon to meet with you." Once she'd arrived at the restaurant, she immediately felt it was worth it to skip class. Colin looked so handsome in his light blue sweater, navy slacks, and navy blue peacoat. His wavy hair always looked tousled, but it only made him look more handsome.

"Well, I'm glad we were able to get together," Colin said, his smile showing perfectly straight white teeth. "I'd prefer dinner with you, but I'll take whatever time I can get."

They ordered lunch and talked for over two hours. Eva enjoyed listening to Colin talking about the bizarre people he met and the funny things they did. He really had an interesting life.

"How do you get away with not working?" Eva asked, then suddenly regretted it. She felt so comfortable with him that she'd just blurted it out. "Sorry. That was rude."

He laughed. "No, it wasn't rude at all. I'm a very lucky man who has a very wealthy father. He bought my apartment and gives me a monthly income. I'm not ashamed to say that. But I do have an eye for art, and I've worked with some of the richest ladies in town to help them find the best pieces for their homes."

"Oh. Sort of like a decorator?" Eva asked.

"Well, not exactly. More like an art connoisseur. I escort rich ladies to galleries, and we discuss the art displays and choose what they love and what I think will be worth money in the future. It's a rather fun game, and they pay me to help them."

"Oh." Eva thought it was an odd job, but at least he didn't just take money from his father. "Is that why you're invited to so many parties?"

"Yes, it is. I've made quite a name for myself." He reached across the table and took her hand in his. "But enough about me. I'd love to spend more time with you. Do you ever go out after you dance? We could go to one of the many holiday parties I've been invited to. Or just spend time together."

"That sounds like fun," Eva said. She'd love to go to a few

parties with him. It was a whole other life she knew nothing about. "I could go out on the nights I don't have a matinee the next day."

Since *The Nutcracker* performances didn't start until Thanksgiving, Eva went out with Colin after rehearsals to the many parties he was invited to. Sometimes they went out to an intimate dinner, and other times they had dinner with large groups of people Eva didn't know. But it was fun. Eva enjoyed spending time with Colin, and to her, that was all that mattered.

On their third date, Colin kissed her under the stars on the balcony of a penthouse apartment with the party music playing softly in the background. It was a chilly, starry night, and it felt magical.

By Thanksgiving, Eva was falling in love with the handsome Colin, and it showed in the glow on her face. At the last dress rehearsal for *The Nutcracker*, Mr. B came up directly to Eva after the snowflake dance and asked her outright.

"Have you been seeing Mr. Sleek?" he asked accusingly. "You are downright glowing."

Eva was taken aback but stood her ground. "I've been seeing Colin," she said, trying not to quiver under his stare. "But it's not interfering with my work."

"Pah!" Mr. B said. "It will, you wait and see. And it will ruin your career as a dancer."

"Wasn't I good in the rehearsal?" Eva asked, suddenly scared he'd take away her lead part in the flower waltz.

Mr. B waved his hand through the air. "Yes. You are perfect. Make sure you stay that way. Don't let Mr. Sleek ruin you."

Eva sighed with relief as Mr. B walked away. She had to be sure to stay rested and dance well throughout the holiday season now that Mr. B was watching her closely.

On Thanksgiving, Eva was invited to Ginny's parents' place for dinner, but she begged off, using the next day's performance as her excuse. Instead, she had dinner in Colin's beautiful apartment in the historic building, The Alden, across from Central Park. It was the first time she'd been there, and Eva was stunned by the grand lobby and how spacious Colin's apartment was. With three bedrooms, two bathrooms, a large living room, and a kitchen, it felt like a house rather than a New York apartment.

He'd ordered a full Thanksgiving dinner for two, and they ate until they were full, then ate pumpkin pie on top of that. Then they cuddled on his comfy sofa by the fire until she felt warm and sleepy.

"I really should go home," Eva said lazily, but not moving at all.

Colin was quiet for a moment, then kissed her on the top of the head. "Don't go. Stay with me tonight," he said softly.

A warm feeling ran through Eva. She was twenty years old, had been working as a dancer since she was sixteen, and had never had a boyfriend or slept with a man. She felt scared and excited all at once. Colin was twenty-six and worldly. Would he think she was too inexperienced and find her silly?

"I want to," she said. "But I'm also scared."

He kissed her again and pulled her closer in his arms. "You don't have to be scared of me. I adore you. I worship you. I promise I won't force myself on you in any way. You can lead the way."

Eva thought about the dancers talking about sex and how great it was. It wasn't something she took lightly, but then, she was so attracted to Colin, she finally understood how it felt to want to be closer. She turned in his arms and kissed him fully.

"I'll stay," she whispered. By morning, she didn't regret her decision.

* * *

The next evening found Eva backstage, watching the acts of *The Nutcracker* that came before the snowflake dance. Her heart was pounding with excitement. The theater was packed, and she knew her Aunt Bea, Uncle Roger, Ginny, and Marty were all in the audience, waiting to see her dance her solo as Dewdrop. Colin was out there, too, in one of the best seats in the house. He'd sent a bouquet of roses to her dressing room before the ballet began.

"My, aren't you the lucky girl," one of the other soloists had said, admiring the roses. "Are they from your boyfriend?"

"Yes," Eva said proudly. "He's in the audience tonight."

The girl smiled at her. "He's a keeper. Roses are expensive." She winked and left to dress for the stage.

Eva thought he was a keeper, too. After spending the night with him last night, she was more than smitten. She was in love.

Eva's mother and stepfather also sent flowers with a lovely note. Her mother wished she could be there, but they were busy at their newly remodeled home and enjoying their first winter in Minnesota. Eva missed her mother but was also happy for her.

That night, Eva danced as if on air. She sailed through the snowflake dance, then rushed to dress for her next performance. Her costume for Dewdrop was short, light pink, and decorated with crystals so she'd sparkle under the lights. She wore a crystal headpiece as well. Once Eva was dressed, she stood in the wings, waiting, her heart beating madly.

"You will be amazing," Mr. B said, coming to stand beside her. She turned and saw the kind smile on his face. "You always are. So, just go out there and shine."

And Eva did. It felt like an out-of-body experience as she fluttered on stage and danced with everything she had. Her feet hurt and her ankles felt like rubber, but she didn't feel any of that. She flew and danced across the stage, and it wasn't until the very end, when the music stopped, that she heard the crowd cheer.

She'd never felt as alive as she did in that moment.

Backstage again, she quickly changed and went to watch the rest of the ballet from the wings. Over the next few weeks, she'd be dancing in this incredible holiday ballet, and she looked forward to every performance. She also couldn't wait to spend more time with Colin.

After the ballet, she met with her family, and Colin also appeared at her side.

"You danced beautifully," Ginny said excitedly. "I'm so proud of you."

"We're all proud of you," Bea said. "I wish your mother were here to see you."

She introduced Colin to her family, and they stood in the lobby for a while and talked. Soon, the place was nearly empty, so they all went their separate ways.

"Let's celebrate with a late dinner," Colin said as they walked outside into the chilly night air. They were both bundled up in coats. "Then, maybe you'll come back to my place?" He looked at her hopefully.

Eva laughed. "I'll have to stop by my apartment first and

get a change of clothes," she said. "I have warm-ups tomorrow morning and another performance at two, then eight again."

"My goodness! They work you to death," Colin said.

"No. It's a privilege to dance this ballet," Eva said.

Colin shrugged as they walked the few blocks to her small apartment. Stepping inside, Colin looked around with wide eyes. "It's a bit small, isn't it?"

"Compared to your place, yes," Eva said, looking around and trying to see it from his perspective. "But it's all I can afford. My mother and I both lived here for years."

"Really?"

Eva chuckled. "When it's all you know, you don't think about it." She found a small bag and put clean clothes, toiletries, and dance clothes into it.

Colin pulled her close and kissed her. "Does this mean you'll stay the night?"

She smiled. "Yes."

They went to a lovely restaurant for dinner, then took a cab to Colin's place. After her exciting evening, Eva was tired, and Colin understood. They spent the night in each other's arms on his comfortable bed. Eva had loved making love to Colin the night before, but just holding each other was also special. She felt safe and warm in his arms.

Throughout the holiday season, Eva and Colin were inseparable. She danced the evening shows, and sometimes the matinees, and he took her to expensive dinners or luxurious holiday parties at penthouses across the city. They enjoyed dinner one night at a famous celebrity's home and another night at the home of a wealthy businessman. All the older, stylish women adored Colin and grew to accept Eva on his arm. She was a ballerina—one of George Balanchine's dancers—and that impressed the elite socialites.

Christmas Eve, they spent the evening at her Aunt Bea's house. Bea and her husband were gracious to Colin, making him feel like family. To everyone's surprise, Marty proposed on bended knee to Ginny, right in front of the sparkling Christmas tree. Ginny clasped her hands together in glee and said yes, and everyone clapped and cheered. Then she slipped on the diamond ring Marty had offered her. It was the perfect ending to a beautiful holiday.

"That's what every woman wants, isn't it?" Colin asked Eva as they rode in a cab back to his apartment. "A fairy-tale marriage proposal and a happily ever after?"

Eva studied his handsome face for a moment, wondering if he was being serious or sarcastic. "That's what Ginny wanted," she finally said. "All I ever wanted to do was dance."

He looked at her, surprised. "You don't want to get married?"

"Maybe. Someday. When it's right," she said.

"You are a one-in-a-million girl," Colin said, kissing her.

Eva was confused by his words but didn't say anything. Yes, she did want to marry someday. But she also remembered Mr. B's warnings about losing interest in dancing once she married. Eva never wanted to give up dancing.

On New Year's Eve, Colin took her to a party at the famous building, The Dakota. "The place is amazing," Colin said as they rode in a cab. "It was built in the late 1800s and is unlike anything else in New York City. And only the very wealthiest and famous people are approved by the board to live there."

"I've never heard you so impressed over an apartment building before," Eva said. "It must be amazing."

"This is no regular apartment building," Colin said. "It's living history."

They walked into the grand lobby and took the elevator up to the seventh floor. A famous actress lived there, known for her roles as a silly blonde. Eva thought she couldn't be as dumb as she portrayed to be able to afford a gorgeous place such as this.

They were greeted by the hostess in the large foyer, where many of the sparkling guests were milling around. A large chandelier hung in the center, its light glittering off the mirror over a wood-paneled fireplace.

"My goodness," Eva said, looking around in awe. "Look at how tall the ceilings are. This place is gorgeous."

"We're just in the entryway," Colin said, laughing.

"Oh, you're the ballerina!" the hostess said, smiling at Eva. "You're so beautiful. I just saw you in *The Nutcracker* over the holidays. You dance beautifully."

"Thank you." Eva felt a warm blush rise to her cheeks. She was looking at the lovely, silver-blonde woman whose curvy figure was clad in white satin. To be called beautiful by a woman like her was a big compliment.

"And Colin, dear," the woman said, smiling widely. "How did you catch this shooting star? If you're not careful, she will float away from you, like a fairy."

"I am a lucky man," Colin said, smiling.

"Please go and mingle. We've opened our doors tonight, and my neighbors are all going to be here. Have a great time, dears," the woman said before turning to her next guest.

They followed a long hallway that led to the dining room and living room. They walked around among the many people and waiters offering drinks and hors d'oeuvres until they reached a large window that overlooked Central Park. The sky was inky black, and the stars shone brightly around the nearly full moon.

"It doesn't get any better than this, does it?" Colin asked, taking two classes of champagne from a waiter and handing one to Eva.

"No, it doesn't," Eva said, starstruck by both the view and the people in the room. She'd never dreamed of a life like this, meeting famous people or standing in iconic buildings. Or being in love with the most handsome man there.

"I love you, Eva," Colin said softly, pulling her close. "I'm so lucky to have you by my side."

Eva snuggled closer. "I love you, too," she said. They clinked glasses for good luck, luck that Eva hoped would follow them throughout a lifetime.

Chapter Nineteen

Eva – 1963

With the holiday season over, the dancers had a break in performing until mid-January. But that didn't mean they had nothing to do. They were back in classes each day and rehearsing a whole new set of dances for the season.

Mr. B had been pleased with Eva's performance as Dewdrop and gave her longer solos and asked her to carefully watch two of the important roles danced by one of the female principals. Eva knew this was big. He hadn't told her to learn the dances, just to watch, but that meant he was considering moving her up to be a principal dancer. She was excited and scared all at once. Would she be ready when he finally did move her up?

She didn't say anything to her fellow dancers because so many of them were easily jealous. She'd watched as Mr. B's new favorite dancer was being spurned by the other dancers because she moved up quickly from a soloist to a principal in only a year. Eva didn't want to cause a stir until her own promotion actually happened. Eva had been a soloist for two years, so it wouldn't be unusual for her to move up. Still, jealousy in the company could be difficult.

And Eva didn't want to do anything that would ruin the happiness she'd found with Colin. By now, she'd practically moved into his apartment. She was still paying rent on her own apartment, and did stay there occasionally when Colin had to be gone overnight for business. But otherwise, she slept each night at Colin's place, and they were still happily in love with each other.

One chilly January morning, as she finished dressing for ballet class and bundled up in her coat to leave, Colin came out of the bathroom, freshly showered with a towel wrapped around his waist.

"Would you drop off a small package for me on your way to class this morning?" he asked casually. "You'll be walking right past the business my friend owns."

"Of course," Eva said. "I'd be happy to."

Colin dug through a dresser drawer and pulled out a small box wrapped in brown paper. The address was written on the box. "I've been meaning to drop this off and keep forgetting," he said. "It's a small statue he asked me to bid on at an auction I went to one afternoon last month, and he's anxious to get it."

Eva took the package. It wasn't heavy, so she figured the statue was small. "I'll drop it off," she said, giving him a quick kiss, then heading off.

Colin lived on Central Park West, and it was about a twenty-minute walk to SAB and Lincoln Center. Most days, Eva chose to walk because it was a good way to warm up her muscles before class. On the coldest or snowiest days, she took a cab. It was an extravagance for her to pay cab fare, but worth it to be with Colin.

She walked along the trail beside Central Park, keeping her

eye out for the street she needed to turn onto to drop off the package. When she saw the street, she quickly crossed over and walked a few feet down. Here, small boutique-style businesses were set up for their high-end clients. Just as she reached the address on the package, she saw a man in an overcoat placing his key in the door to open it. When he saw Eva, he turned and smiled. His hair was silver and wavy, and he had a kind face. Eva smiled back.

"Are you John Earlington?" she asked.

"Why, yes, dear. I am," he said pleasantly. "You must be the ballerina. I was just opening up my business."

She handed him the small package. "I'm on my way to dance class, so I have to run. It was nice meeting you, Mr. Earlington."

"My pleasure, dear," John said, clutching the package. "Say hello to Colin for me."

She nodded and headed back in the direction that she'd come.

Class had already begun as Eva arrived, so she hurried to tie up her pointe shoes and join them. She received a few stares, but no one said anything as she melded seamlessly into the class. Later, as the dancers stretched and headed to their rehearsals, a thin shadow fell over Eva. She glanced up, and there stood Mr. B.

"You were late to class, again," he said in his soft voice. He was neither scolding her nor angry with her. "Is Mr. Sleek keeping you up late at night?"

Eva stood. "I'm sorry, Mr. B. I had an errand to run and didn't think it would make me late." The last thing she wanted to do was make Balanchine angry at her. He'd been so generous to her with roles and her career, but he could take it all away if he lost interest in her.

"You didn't answer my question, dear. Are you still going out about town with Mr. Sleek?"

Eva sighed. "His name is Colin, and yes, we've been dating. He's very kind to me."

"Hm." Mr. B sniffed, as he always did when he found something distasteful. "Remember what I always say, dear. Men will ruin your career. Dance should always come first."

Eva smiled. She knew Mr. B was just looking out for her as he'd always done. From the time she was a child, walking home in the dark, he made sure she was safe. She couldn't blame him for continuing to worry about her. "Dancing does come first. It always will," she reassured him.

"Good." He nodded his head. "Now, off to rehearsal. You have dances to perfect."

Eva hurried off. She had solos in two ballets starting in mid-January, and although she knew them well, she also knew she could always do better.

* * *

That spring was an exciting time at the ballet company. Mr. B was filled with inspiration and was creating new ballets for his principal dancers. Although Eva was a soloist, she was asked to be one of six women to dance in the background for a ballet titled *Movements*. The ballet featured Jacques and Diana Adams, so Eva was thrilled to be in this new, unique style of ballet. The ballet was to premiere in April, and Eva rehearsed each day with the other women to make it perfect.

One evening, as Eva was in the soloist's dressing room, preparing for the first of the two dances she performed, she heard the girls whispering about some scandalous news.

"She didn't know when the jewels were stolen. After her New Year's Eve party, she'd left for a month to Paris, and when she returned, they were gone," one girl said as if she had first-hand knowledge.

Eva's ears perked up. New Year's Eve party? It couldn't possibly be the one she'd attended. "Who are you talking about?" Eva asked. "What happened?"

"Don't you watch the news or read the papers?" the gossipy girl asked. "It's all over everything."

Eva didn't own a television set and had no time to read the papers. "No. Tell me."

The girl was all too happy to tell her again about a famous actress whose jewelry was stolen right out of her apartment at The Dakota. "They're keeping her name anonymous, but we've been trying to guess who she is. Only the richest and most successful people live in The Dakota."

Eva frowned. "Someone stole her jewelry?"

"Yes," the girl said, sounding annoyed. "Didn't you hear me? She thinks it might actually be one of her neighbors since she'd opened her apartment to everyone on New Year's Eve. Can you imagine? Or, it could have been that sneaky cat burglar who's been going around town stealing jewelry right out from under the rich women's noses. People have been speculating for over a year who is doing that."

"Cat burglar?" Eva hadn't heard of any of this before. But she knew whose jewels had been stolen from The Dakota, because it had to be the woman who hosted the New Year's Eve party they attended. It was scary to think that someone in that room was a thief.

After she danced that night, Eva took a cab back to Colin's

apartment and was surprised that he wasn't home. He'd said he had a meeting with one of his rich lady friends to attend a new art show and help her pick out something for her apartment. By the time Eva was changed for bed, having washed off all her stage makeup and pulled her hair down from its bun, Colin walked in looking tired.

"Ah, sweetheart! It's so wonderful to see you after the evening I've had," Colin said in his charming English accent. He fell on the bed and curled up next to her. "The very rich have the worst taste. I suggested wonderful pieces from the show to that woman, and she kept returning to the ugliest pieces in the room. She finally bought the ugliest painting I've ever seen. I certainly hope she doesn't tell anyone I helped her pick it out. It's horrendous!"

Eva smiled as he spoke. She loved how animated he got when he had a bad or good day helping his rich friends. His stories always made her laugh. But tonight, she had a lot on her mind.

"What's wrong? Did you have a bad performance tonight?" He asked, reaching up and curling a strand of her red hair behind her ear.

"No. I'm just tired," she said.

He kissed her, then pushed himself off the bed and took off his suit jacket. "I can't wait to get undressed and crawl into bed with you. Do you have an early morning tomorrow?"

"I have an early morning every day except Sundays," she said.

"True, true," he called out from the bathroom where he was brushing his teeth.

"The girls in the dressing room tonight were talking about a jewelry theft over at The Dakota recently," Eva said. "I think it happened to the woman whose party we attended."

Colin came out of the bathroom wearing a T-shirt and boxer shorts. "Really? I hadn't heard about that. You'd think my rich friend tonight would have been gossiping about it."

"The girls said there's been a cat burglar stealing jewelry around town for almost a year. Isn't that weird? The police haven't been able to figure out who it is," Eva said.

"Interesting," Colin said, then returned to the bathroom to finish his teeth. He came out and slid into bed beside Eva. "So, who do you think this cat burglar is?"

Eva shrugged. "I don't know. Have you heard about these thefts before? You have many rich women friends. It seems like they would have talked about it."

"I've seen something in the newspaper," Colin said. "But no one has mentioned it. These socialites are usually self-involved and don't care what's happening to anyone else."

Eva smiled. "That's true. I find it odd, though. We were in the very apartment right before it was robbed. It gives me chills. What if the thief was there that night? We may have even talked to him."

"Or her," Colin said.

Eva's brows shot up. "I didn't even think it could be a woman. I suppose it could be."

"It could be anyone," Colin said. "It could be me. Or you." He tickled her under the covers.

Eva laughed. "Don't be silly."

"Well, I wouldn't worry about a cat burglar coming here," Colin said. "We don't have much to steal. Unless some secret admirer of yours has given you diamonds or emeralds."

"Sorry. The only admirer I have is you."

Colin shook his head. "That's a shame. A beauty like you

should have hundreds of men waiting at the stage door just for you."

Eva smiled. "I don't want them. I only want you." She kissed him deeply, and all talk ceased for the rest of the night.

* * *

The season continued. By the time *Movements* premiered, Diana had been replaced by Balanchine's latest favorite dancer because Diana had learned she was pregnant, and she didn't want to risk a miscarriage. Eva loved dancing in the background for *Movements*. The dance style was so different from what she was used to, with stances being more geometrical and movements jerky. But it was also beautiful, and the audience loved it. Once again, Mr. B had created a stunning new ballet.

Eva and Colin continued to attend glamours receptions, birthday parties, dinner parties, and other events. They even attended a party given by a patron of the New York City Ballet, along with the other dancers, at the end of the dance season. Mr. B was polite to Colin, but he still didn't like him. He told Eva that Colin was too "sleek" for his taste. Eva could only laugh it off.

Eva occasionally dropped off small packages to John Earlington on her way to dance class. She didn't mind. If it saved Colin some time, she was happy to do it. She was, however, curious about what kind of statues Mr. Earlington purchased that were so small. Colin mentioned they were the size of chess pieces. She guessed he had a collection of small pieces.

At the end of the season, Eva was asked if she'd like to join the dance company in California for a summer tour. She was thrilled to be invited. They'd be dancing the ballets she already knew, so she wouldn't have to learn anything new. She took class daily and did rehearsals all summer anyway, to stay in shape. She couldn't wait to go to California. Even though she'd lived there as a child, she didn't remember much about it.

"Do you think you could come along, even for a short time?" she asked Colin one evening. "We'll be in Los Angeles and San Francisco. Either town would be fun."

"I'd love to come along," Colin said. "But I'll have to check my schedule. There are a few art openings during that time, and I have one lady who'd like me to help her find art for her home in the Hamptons."

Eva sighed. "I wish you could come along. But I know you're busy. Maybe, if you get a chance, you can sneak a flight there one weekend."

Colin gave her one of his dashing smiles. "You know I will if I'm able. I dread thinking of you being gone for two months."

In June, Colin escorted Eva to Ginny and Martin's wedding, which was held in a sweet neighborhood church with a reception at Bea's apartment. Ginny looked so grown-up in a white suit and heels, and Martin was handsome in a black suit. Ginny hadn't wanted a big white-dress wedding because she was too sensible for that. She decided she'd rather spend the money on an apartment for herself and Martin rather than on a wedding for three hundred people.

Eva handed Ginny an envelope that Mr. B had given her for the new bride. When Ginny opened it, she was surprised. Mr. B had given her a beautiful wedding card and fifty dollars. It said, *I hope you both are very happy for decades to come.*

"I thought Mr. Balanchine didn't believe in marriage," Ginny said. "This was so thoughtful of him."

Eva laughed. "He doesn't believe in his dancers getting married and having children. But he definitely believes in marriage."

Ginny nodded toward Colin, who was charming several of Bea's friends across the room. "Will you be getting married soon, too? You two have been living together for a while."

"I'm not sure," Eva said, but grinned. "And I do still have my own apartment. But I wouldn't say no if he asked."

That summer, Eva and Colin enjoyed their time together in between Eva's practice days and the summer session she helped teach at SAB. Eva had never been happier, spending her nights with Colin. They still attended parties and openings, but fewer this time of year. It was hot in the city, and most of the upper class had gone to Newport, the Hamptons, and Martha's Vineyard. August came too quickly, and soon Eva would be off to Los Angeles with the dancers and Mr. B to perform at the Greek Theater.

"I wish you could come, too," Eva said, feeling sad about leaving Colin behind. She was packing her bag for the flight the next day. "I'll miss you."

"I'll miss you, too, sweetie. But I have something for you." He opened a dresser drawer and pulled out a narrow, long box. "Maybe this will help you remember me while you're gone."

Eva's heart pounded. She knew it had to be jewelry—the first he'd ever given her. She opened the velvet box and inside lay a beautiful one-carat round diamond on a sparkling gold chain.

"Oh, it's beautiful!" she exclaimed. "I love it!"

"Here. Let me put it on you." Colin lifted the necklace from the box and clasped it behind her neck. "It's perfect."

Eva lifted her hand so her fingers could touch the lovely

diamond. It sparkled in the light as she stared into the mirror over the dresser. "It is perfect." She turned and wrapped her arms around his neck. "Thank you so much!"

"You deserve so much more, sweetie," Colin whispered in her ear. "This is just the first of many beautiful gems for you."

She pulled back and stared into his blue eyes. "I love it, but I love you more. You're all I need."

"I love hearing that." Colin lifted her up in his arms and twirled her around. "I'll always love hearing that."

The next day, Colin rode in the taxi with Eva to the airport. "Don't forget me while you're gone," he said. "I'll be here, helping old ladies pick out ridiculously priced paintings."

"And I'll be dancing in the city of angels wearing a sparkling diamond my boyfriend gave me," Eva said.

"Oh, I forgot." Colin pulled a box out of his blazer pocket. "While you're in Los Angeles, can you stop at this address and deliver this package. Your hotel, The Ambassador, is just down the street from there."

Eva took the package from him and looked at the address. It was on Wilshire Boulevard, just as their hotel was. "Uh, sure. Okay." She frowned at Colin. "What's inside?"

"Oh, just a collectible a gentleman asked me to pick up from an estate sale," Colin said offhandedly. "I could have mailed it, but I was afraid it would get lost, and it's very valuable."

"Colin?" she asked tentatively. She'd never questioned the packages he'd asked her to deliver before, but this made her nervous. She'd be going across country, and if there was something nefarious in the package, she didn't want to get caught with it. "Is it…legal?"

Colin's brows shot up. "Legal? Of course, it's legal," he said, looking shocked. "I'd never ask you to deliver anything you'd get in trouble for." Then he chuckled. "It's not drugs or anything like that. It's all on the up and up."

Eva sighed. "Okay. I'm just a little nervous taking it across country, that's all."

"Don't be, sweetie. It's a collectible, that's all. Trust me."

They said goodbye at the gate, and Mr. B hung back to walk Eva onto the plane. He always made sure every last dancer got on safely.

"So, you're still seeing Mr. Sleek, I see," Mr. B said as they boarded the plane. "I hope he is worth it."

Eva looked over at Mr. B. "He's good to me," she said. "We love each other."

Mr. B nodded. "You deserve the best, dear. That's all I'm saying." They separated as they took their seats, and Eva sat down next to another dancer. She'd stuffed the box Colin had given her into her bag. Despite how much she loved Colin, Eva had a terrible feeling that the small box could get her into deep trouble.

Chapter Twenty

Maddie

Maddie stood at the island in the kitchen, staring nervously at her mother's laptop. The ACT scores were out, and all she had to do was look online to see how she'd done. She couldn't get up the nerve to do it, though.

"What are you waiting for?" Lily asked, annoyed. "Look it up. Don't you want to know your score?"

"I do," Maddie said. "I'm just scared I may have failed."

Sandy walked into the house from her morning session, practicing at Eva's house. "What's going on?"

"Maddie's too chicken to look up her ACT score," Lily blurted out.

"Oh, are they out? Let's have a look," Sandy said excitedly.

"But what if I did poorly?" Maddie asked. "I couldn't stand it if I didn't do well. Livie just called and said she got a twenty-seven. What if I didn't at least get that?"

"Oh, honey," Sandy said, wrapping her arms around Maddie from behind. "I'm sure you did fine. But we won't know if we don't look."

Maddie lifted the screen and signed in, then entered the URL for the ACT scores. The page popped up and flickered at her as she stared at it. All she had to do was enter her password to see her score. But she couldn't get her fingers to work.

"Let me do it," Lily said, nudging Maddie aside. "What's your password?"

Maddie told her and watched as Lily typed it in. The page popped up, and there, in front of her, were her scores for each section and her average score.

It was a twenty-nine.

"Oh, my goodness!" Sandy screamed. "You did great! Twenty-nine is way above average."

Maddie let out the breath she'd been holding in. She'd done well. Thank goodness!

Lily and Sandy were jumping up and down, and Maddie joined in.

"See. It wasn't so bad," Lily said. "But you didn't get a perfect score."

Maddie rolled her eyes. "Leave it to you to bring that up. But it's still a high score. High enough to get a partial academic scholarship at some colleges. And if I can keep a 4.0 grade average next year, I might get an even better scholarship."

"Our college offers a good academic scholarship," Sandy said. "I had half my college paid for. And since you'll be taking a couple of college courses in your senior year, that will help, too."

Maddie grew quiet. She didn't have the heart to ruin the moment for her mother by telling her she was thinking of going away to college.

That night at dinner, Maddie proudly told her father her ACT score, and he gave her a high-five.

"That's great, Mads," Matt said. "I'm so proud of you. It will help financially, too. The local college is great for scholarships."

"Maybe Maddie doesn't want to go to college here," Lily said. She scooped up a mouthful of mashed potatoes. "I know I won't be going to college here, either."

Matt and Sandy both stared at Maddie.

"We have to see where I'm accepted first," Maddie said quickly. "I'll definitely apply here, just in case."

"In case of what?" Matt asked, placing his fork down on his plate. "I thought you were going to school here. They have an excellent teacher's program."

Maddie picked at her food, not wanting to answer him. She knew her parents had their hearts set on her staying at home during college. "I've just been looking at a few options, that's all," Maddie said.

"Mads, tell them the truth," Lily said. "Livie is going to apply to the University of Denver. She's been offered a spot on the gymnastics team, so she'll probably get a full scholarship. Maddie wants to go there, too."

"Lily!" Maddie said. "You don't know what's going on."

"Yes, I do," Lily said. "Livie was telling me about it. Why is it a secret? It's what you want to do."

"Is that what you want to do?" Sandy asked, looking at Maddie.

"I'm not sure what I want right now," Maddie said. "I'm going to apply to a couple of places, that's all. It's a whole year away." She just wanted to get the attention off of her, and fast!

"What does DU have that our college doesn't?" Matt asked. "I mean, if you're going to be a teacher."

Maddie interrupted him. "Dad. I'm not sure I want to be a teacher. I want to go to school for creative writing. DU has a great writing program. Better than our local college." She let out a breath. There! She'd said it.

"That's going to be really expensive," Matt said. "You know out-of-state tuition is twice as much as in-state. And all for what? To get a degree in something you can't even get a job with after graduation. Who hires creative writers? Now, if you wanted to teach writing or English, that would make more sense."

"I don't want to teach!" Maddie stood up, and her silverware clattered on her plate. "You aren't listening to me, Dad. I don't want to be a teacher. I want to write."

"Maddie, sweetie, please sit down and let's talk this over calmly," Sandy said.

"I don't want to talk about it at all," Maddie said. "I'm going up to my room." She ran up the stairs and into her room, closing the door quietly behind her.

Tears filled Maddie's eyes as she fell onto her bed. Why didn't her father understand that she wanted to do something different from his expectations? There was nothing wrong with being a teacher, but she didn't want to be one. All she wanted to do was write.

Wiping her eyes, she sat up in bed and pulled out the notebook she was writing Eva's story in. The last time she was over there, Eva had stopped her story when she got on the plane to California. Eva was only a few years older than Maddie was now, but she did exciting things and was already in love with a great guy. And no one was telling her what to do. Well, except for Mr. B, but he was just looking out for her. Maddie sighed. She knew her father was trying to look out for her, too. But why did parents always think that they knew better than their kids?

A soft knock came on Maddie's door, and her shoulders sagged. The last thing she wanted to do was fight with her parents again.

The door opened, and Sandy stuck her head inside the room. "Hey. Can we talk?"

Maddie nodded, closing her notebook and setting it aside.

"Is that the notebook with Eva's story in it?" Sandy asked.

"Yes. I was going to add the latest part of the story that Eva told me."

"Eva had an interesting life. I wish I'd heard the latest part of her story, but I can always read it when you're finished writing about it," Sandy said.

"Mom. About earlier," Maddie began, but Sandy interrupted her.

"Don't worry about earlier," she said. "I talked with your dad, and he now understands that you might need to go away to college to follow your dream."

Maddie's brows shot up. "How did you change his mind?"

Sandy smiled. "I reminded him that it's taken me years to finally find my dream again. And I don't want you to have to wait that long to find yours."

Maddie felt a knot in her throat. Her mother did understand. "Thanks."

Sandy placed her hand over Maddie's. "I want you to find what makes you happy, dear. Life is too long—and too short to be unhappy. You do what you think is best."

"I'm not even sure where I'll end up yet," Maddie said. "I'll apply to a few places and see what happens."

Sandy stood. "You do what you have to do. Meanwhile, I'm still working on getting back into dancing shape to teach this fall. I can't believe how excited I am to do this." She paused.

"You gave me a gift, bringing me there again," she told Maddie. "A wonderful gift."

Maddie stood and hugged her mother as tears fell down her cheeks. She was so happy her mother found dancing again, and she hoped she'd find her way to the thing that made her that happy, too.

After a time, they parted, and both women wiped their eyes.

"I have chocolate cake for dessert," Sandy said. "Store-bought, but it's still good. We'd better get a piece before your dad and Lily eat it all."

Maddie nodded, and they went downstairs together. When she met her father's eyes, he smiled.

"You do what you have to do, sweetie," he told her when she sat on the sofa with a piece of cake. "You know me, always a stickler for being practical. But I get it. You know, I wanted to be a baseball star when I grew up. But it was just a dream."

"I didn't know that," Maddie said. She knew her father played baseball in high school, but he didn't play in college.

"Well, I didn't make the college team, and I had to concentrate on my studies. It's not that I don't like my job, because I do. But yeah. It would have been fun to play ball all my life."

Maddie smiled, trying to picture her father as a college freshman, embarking on his life without being able to do the thing he loved. She hoped that wouldn't happen to her. As long as writing was her passion, she hoped she'd be able to do it for years to come.

* * *

The next day, Maddie knocked on Eva's door. She no longer made the excuse that their lawn needed mowing. She knew she was welcome to come there anytime, and she couldn't wait for Eva to tell her more of her story.

"You just can't stay away," Ginny said with a grin as she let her in. "It must be my amazing cooking skills."

"I do love your lunches," Maddie said.

"Auck! You love Eva's story more. Come along, she's in the big room, reminiscing. I'll make enough for the three of us for lunch."

Maddie stood at the threshold of the big room and watched Eva sitting in a chair, staring at one of the large pictures of herself on the wall. It was the one where Eva was posing in arabesque, her pointe shoe on the floor in the perfect ballerina arch. It was a breathtaking picture, and Maddie wondered if Eva was thinking of the day it was taken.

As if sensing Maddie behind her, Eva spoke softly. "That photo was taken by the company photographer in Los Angeles during our California tour in 1963," she said, her voice sounding dreamy. "A few months later, my life changed forever."

Maddie walked up behind her and placed her hands on Eva's shoulders. "I'd love to hear more of your story."

Eva nodded. "Come. Sit, and I'll tell you more."

Maddie walked around Eva and sat in one of the cushy chairs that stood in the middle of the living room. Soon, these chairs and the sofa would be moved to make room for little girls who wanted to learn ballet from her mother.

"The tour in California was so much fun, despite Colin not coming along," Eva said. "As a group, we visited Disneyland and Knott's Berry Farm. We drove a rented car around Beverly Hills and Bel Air, gazing at the beautiful mansions where the stars lived. We also went to the beach several times and tanned, even though Mr. B hated it when we did that. He wanted us all to have pale skin because it looked like alabaster under the stage lights." She laughed. "We used a lot of white powder to cover our arms and chest when we were on stage. It was one of the best summers of my life, yet underneath all the dancing and sightseeing, I couldn't help but feel a sinister foreboding deep down inside of me. I had no idea why."

Chapter Twenty-One

Eva – 1963

Eva and the other dancers loved California. It was warm, but not hot, like New York's steamy summers. They wore sundresses during the day as they went sightseeing and shopping, then danced to sold-out performances at the Greek Theater at night. Dancing in the evening at the outdoor venue was an experience all its own. Eva learned quickly to smile, but keep her mouth shut, or else she might accidentally swallow a curious insect flying toward the stage lights. But the crowds made up for a few little inconveniences. They clapped gleefully after each dance and kept coming back for more.

While in Los Angeles, Mr. B was invited to several luxurious homes by celebrities who loved the ballet. He brought along his favorite dancers, including Eva. She met movie stars, musicians, and television personalities, most of whom were polite and interested in what the dancers had to say. It was an exciting experience for the young dancers, but they knew better than to let it all go to their heads. Everyone showed up each morning for class and stage rehearsals and danced each night for the crowds.

After a few days in L.A., Eva reluctantly walked the short distance from their hotel to the address Colin had written on the package she was asked to deliver. The traffic on Wilshire Boulevard was buzzing all day long, but there were sidewalks to walk on. She turned onto a street, and tucked away between two office buildings was a small antique jewelry shop that had the address she was looking for painted on a sign above the glass door. Pushing open the door, she walked inside. A middle-aged man in a pinstriped suit with a red tie looked up from behind a glass counter.

"Can I help you, Miss?" he asked.

Eva noticed the man's black hair was stiff with hairspray, and he wore a large, gold ring on his pinky finger. He looked like a gangster from an old 1930s movie. "I have a package from Colin Hughes," she said. "Are you the owner?"

He smiled. "Yes, I am. And I've been expecting you." He tilted his head to the side. "You're the ballerina from the New York City Ballet. Colin told me a pretty girl would drop this off."

Eva smiled back and handed him the package. Something about the man made her uncomfortable, and all she wanted to do was get out of the small shop.

"Thank you, dear," the man said, eyeing the package greedily. "Have a look around. You might see something you like. I'll let Colin know so he can buy it for you."

The bell on the door jingled, and two men in dark suits walked inside. The shop owner's face turned from a smile to a sneer.

"I'd better be going," Eva said quickly. "It was nice meeting you." She hurried past the two men and out the door, walking so quickly that she was nearly to the hotel by the time she realized she was out of breath. She slowed her pace. Eva couldn't get the angry face of the shop owner out of her mind. Right then and there, she vowed she wouldn't make any more deliveries for Colin. Something was wrong, and she didn't want to find out what it was.

The company had as wonderful a time in San Francisco as they'd had in Los Angeles. The audiences were amazing, and they were able to sightsee at Fisherman's Wharf and Chinatown. By the time they all flew out of California, Eva had forgotten about the little shop in Los Angeles. She couldn't wait to go home and see Colin again.

Colin met her at the airport in early September and swung her in his arms as the other dancers walked past with grins on their faces.

"You're making a spectacle of yourselves," Mr. B grumbled as he walked past them. Eva only laughed. She knew Mr. B's anger was directed toward Colin, not her.

"Crabby old man," Colin said with a wide smile on his face. He was just as handsome as ever, wearing a blue cashmere sweater and trousers, his hair waving in all the right places.

"He's just looking out for me," Eva said. "Let's go home."

Colin asked her all about California, and she rattled on about the places they went to and all they saw while there. When the cab drew nearer to Colin's apartment building, he asked her about the box. "Did you deliver my package?"

Eva's excitement waned. "Yes, I did. But I was very uncomfortable doing it. Something felt off about the man and the place."

"I'm sorry," Colin said, hugging her close. "I never meant for you to feel that way."

"Please don't ask me to deliver any more packages," Eva said. "I feel strange doing it, especially when I don't know what's in them."

"I promise, there is nothing nefarious about the packages," Colin said, dropping a kiss on her cheek.

Once home, they forgot all about the strange little packages as Colin welcomed Eva home in the most intimate way.

The NYCB fall season began immediately after the dance company arrived home in New York City. New dancers had been added to the corps de ballet, and there were two new soloists. Everyone had been rehearsing for the new season. Eva expected to continue in the roles she already knew, but was surprised by the ballet mistress on the first day of classes.

"Mr. B would like you to take on two principal roles," she told her, then grinned. "Are you ready to be in the spotlight?"

"Oh, yes!" Eva said, forcing herself not to jump up and down with excitement. "I am so ready."

Eva learned she would be one of two female leads in *Concerto Barocco* and would dance the second movement of the ballet with Jacques. This would be a big step forward in her career. While she'd taken Jacques' classes, she'd never danced with him formally.

Eva's other lead role would be in *Allegro Brillante*. It was a beautiful ballet with quick steps and multiple pirouettes. She would be dancing with another principal male lead in the company, Eddie Villella. While Eva had taken many classes that Eddie also attended, they had never danced together, but she was excited for the chance.

Rehearsals started immediately. Eva had a lot to learn in very little time. This was a pattern with Mr. B and all his dancers. He'd suddenly place them in a role, and they'd have to learn it within a few days. But Eva was up to the challenge, and dancing with two seasoned male dancers in the company helped make learning easier. Both Eddie and Jacques were patient and great teachers. Even as they rehearsed, Eva couldn't believe she was dancing with either of them.

"Oh, I wish I could be there to see you dance as a principal dancer," Eva's mother said over the phone when she called to tell her the good news. "Ray hasn't been feeling well these past few weeks, and I don't want to drag him across the country on a crowded airplane. But I'm so proud of you, dear."

"Thanks, Mom," Eva said, a little disappointed her mother wouldn't see her on stage. "I understand, though. Ray's health is more important."

"Don't worry, Eva," Colin said after she'd hung up. "I'll be there to watch you. And I'm sure Ginny and her new husband will come, too."

Eva smiled. She felt so lucky to have a man like Colin in her life.

The morning of the last rehearsal, Eva was hurrying out of the apartment when Colin caught up with her, a small box in his hand.

"Would you mind dropping this off at Earlington's business before going to class?" Colin asked, a sweet smile on his face. "I know you hate doing this, but I promise, this will be the last time."

Eva frowned down at the small box, then looked up into Colin's light blue eyes. They'd been together for almost a year, and he'd never done anything to make her feel unsafe. But the packages bothered her. "I don't know," she said, indecision in her voice.

"Please?" Colin begged. "I'd do it, but I have to be at an art gallery to meet a client on the other side of town. I wouldn't ask if it weren't important."

Eva was running late, and she didn't have time to quibble over the package. "Okay. But this is the last time."

Colin smiled brightly. "You're a doll." He kissed her lips as she hurried out the door.

Eva shoved the package into her dance bag and hurried out of the building, waving to the doorman as she passed him. She crossed the street to the sidewalk next to Central Park and walked quickly. She wondered what was really in the small packages Colin asked her to deliver. If she had time, she'd stop and open this one to make sure it wasn't something illegal. But she didn't want to be late to Mr. B's class.

Crossing over to the other side again, she walked quickly to John Earlington's shop. As always, he was outside the door, keys in hand.

"Oh, my dear. You always have perfect timing," he said, smiling widely.

People on the sidewalk brushed past them as she reached into her bag and pulled out the box. "I'm late for class," she said. "Here it is." Turning, Eva ran right into two men wearing dark suits and overcoats.

"Oh, sorry," she said, trying to get past them. But the men each grabbed one of her arms.

"You're not going anywhere, Miss," one of the men said.

Eva's heart pounded with fear. She'd heard so many horror stories of people being mugged in NYC, but she'd never thought it would happen to her. She turned her head to look at John for help, but he was also being detained by two men.

The men walked her over to where John was. A fifth man had the box in his hand.

"Now, let's see what's inside," he said, ripping it open. He pulled out some tissue paper and unwrapped it. Lying inside the paper were several pieces of gemstone and diamond jewelry. Bracelets, necklaces, and even a large brooch glittered in the fall sunshine.

Eva forgot about the men holding her and gaped at the jewelry. Was this what she'd been delivering for Colin the entire time? Expensive jewelry? Her mind spun back to the talk of a cat burglar preying on wealthy socialites. The very women whom Colin claimed to help buy art.

"You're coming with us, Miss," one of the men said. "You're under arrest for the transportation of stolen goods."

Arrest? Eva looked up as one of the men was flashing a badge at her. Her heart sank. The man she loved had set her up to take the fall for him.

* * *

Eva sat in a little room at the police precinct for over two hours answering questions. The men who'd arrested her shot out question after question until her head spun. Fortunately, she'd had the presence of mind to give her real name, not her stage name, when they'd arrested her. She hoped that by telling them she was Eve Arthur, her name wouldn't show up in the newspaper as Evalina Ashford, ballerina. The last thing she wanted was for her arrest to stain the reputation of the New York City Ballet, and Mr. B.

"I knew nothing about the robberies," Eva said for the hundredth time. "I swear. I only delivered the packages to John Earllington for my boyfriend because it was on my way to work."

"Yes, we know all about your boyfriend," one of the detectives said. "And you were living in his fancy apartment with him. We've been watching you both for months. It's hard to believe that you didn't know for almost a year how he earned his money."

"But I didn't," Eva said, tears filling her eyes. "He said his father was rich and he worked at helping rich socialites find art for their homes. We went to parties given by those rich women because they all knew him. I had nothing to do with stealing jewelry."

"You can't be that stupid," the other detective said. "Colin Hughes, alias Anthony Rumsey, has been conning people since he was a kid. And that English accent of his? It's phony. He was raised in Michigan, near Detroit. He's no more an English aristocrat than I am."

Eva couldn't believe what she was hearing. She'd fallen in love with a con man who didn't even use his real name. Not only was she frightened over what would become of her, but she was heartbroken as well.

"And what about your little package drop in L.A.?" the first detective asked. "We walked in as you gave it to the shop owner. He's a known dealer of stolen goods. You were caught red-handed."

Eva gasped as she remembered how shady the entire drop-off felt. The man behind the counter had given her the creeps, and then she remembered two men in dark suits entering the shop. She'd had no idea they were cops.

"I didn't know what I was delivering," she said. "I just did it for Colin. I had no reason to believe he was doing anything illegal."

"You took stolen jewelry across state lines," the second

detective said. "That could mean years in prison. Do you understand that?"

Eva's shoulders dropped. She hadn't done anything wrong, but here she was, being threatened with prison time. "I honestly knew nothing," she said in a small voice.

"Well, if you tell us what you do know, we might make a deal with you. Or are you too in *love* with your con-man boyfriend to squeal on him?"

"I'll tell you everything I know, but it's not much," Eva said. Then she had a thought. If she could make a deal with them, she knew exactly what it was going to be.

Two hours later, she was allowed to make a phone call. Eva called her mother in Minnesota.

"Mom?" Eva said, feeling exhausted after her long day. "I need your help."

"Dear. What is it?" Gwen asked.

"Colin isn't the man I thought he was. He's been stealing jewelry from rich women whose parties we attended. I've been arrested." Eva was no longer crying. She'd cried all her tears over Colin's betrayal. Now, she had to think of her future, if she still had one.

"Oh, my goodness, no!" Gwen sounded shocked. "Do you have a lawyer? Ray will know someone we can send over to you."

"I do need a lawyer," Eva said. "But the first thing I need is for you to call Mr. B at his office and talk only to him—no one else. Insist on talking to him. He'll be wondering where I am by now. You need to tell him what happened. I made a deal with the detectives to help them with anything I could in exchange for them not to tell the press my stage name and profession."

"Honey? You shouldn't have made a deal without a lawyer," Gwen said.

"I had to, Mom. Otherwise, tomorrow's papers would have a headline about the cat burglar and his ballerina girlfriend. I can't do that to Mr. B. Not after everything he's done for me all these years."

Gwen sighed. "I understand, dear."

"I'm arrested under my real name, so with any luck, no one will put the pieces together," Eva said. A lump formed in her throat. She had no idea what was going to happen to her, but she couldn't involve Mr. B or the ballet company. "Can you call him, please? And I could use a lawyer if Ray knows any."

"I'll call Mr. B right now," Gwen said. "And then a lawyer. And I'll be on the next plane to New York so I can be there for you."

Tears filled Eva's eyes. "I'm so sorry, Mom," she said softly. "I had no idea what Colin was doing. I feel so stupid."

"Oh, honey," Gwen said, her voice cracking. "You're not the first, nor the last woman to be conned by a man. I'm so sorry."

Eva was sorry, too. Her life as she knew it was over. She was just Eve Arthur, and nothing more. At only twenty-one years old, her dancing career was over.

Chapter Twenty-Two

Maddie

Eva and Maddie sat in silence for a long while after Eva had stopped talking. Maddie was shocked at what had happened to her, and Eva was visibly exhausted after telling her.

"Do you think any less of me, dear?" Eva finally said, lifting her eyes to Maddie's.

"No, of course not!" Maddie exclaimed. "You were innocent. Colin was the guilty one."

"Yes, he was," Eva said. "Unfortunately, I was an accessory to his crimes. I was so naïve that I didn't realize someone could tell you they loved you and then use you that way. It was heartbreaking."

"I'm so sorry that happened to you," Maddie said, calmer now. "Did you go to jail? Did they ever arrest Colin?"

Ginny had been listening from the doorway. "I think Eva has said enough for one day," she said gently. "Let's lighten things up by enjoying lunch."

"Oh, of course." Maddie felt guilty for pushing Eva to continue. She had seen the worn look on Eva's face and knew reliving those memories had been hard for her.

They ate Ginny's delicious grilled cheese sandwiches along with carrot sticks and iced tea. Eva's color returned after she'd eaten and her mood had lifted.

"I did well on my ACTs," Maddie told the ladies after lunch. "Once I apply to schools, I can find out if they'll give me any scholarships for academics."

"Oh, that's wonderful!" Eva said, clapping her hands with glee. "Where are you going to apply?"

"I'll apply to the college here, because my parents want me to. And I also want to apply to the University of Denver. They have an excellent creative writing program. I may also apply to the University of Minnesota in Minneapolis. It's not my first choice, though. But if Livie decides to go there, I will, too."

"You're gymnast friend, Olivia?" Ginny asked.

"Yes," Maddie said. She hadn't mentioned Livie before. "How did you know?"

"Your mother has spoken of her," Ginny said. "It's wonderful to have a friend to go off to school with, but you need to choose the best place for you."

Maddie nodded. "I wish my parents understood that. I know my mother will support me no matter where I go, but my dad is having a hard time understanding that I don't want to be an English teacher. He doesn't see writing as a way to earn money."

"He'll come around, dear," Eva said. "I'm sure he's having a hard time accepting that his little girl is grown up and will leave home in a year."

Maddie smiled. "Yes, I suppose." She looked at her phone and sighed. "I have a shift at the Freeze soon, so I guess I'd better go home and change. Thanks for the delicious lunch, Ginny."

Ginny waved her hand through the air to brush aside her compliment. "Any time, dear. You're always welcome."

Eva walked Maddie to the door.

"Thank you for telling me more of your story today," Maddie said. "I can't wait to write it down. If you'd like me to keep it confidential, I will."

Eva smiled. "I've never told anyone about being arrested in all these years. Only my family and Mr. B knew. It's actually a relief to finally have it out in the open."

"Thank you for trusting me," Maddie said, her heart swelling with love for Eva. After everything she'd told her this summer, Maddie felt like they were connected. She hugged Eva before walking out the door. Turning, Maddie asked, "May I come here tomorrow to hear the rest of your story?"

Eva nodded. "Yes. Please do. I'm looking forward to it."

Maddie left, feeling lighthearted. She didn't mind going to work tonight, even if she had to work with Carrie. They were getting along well now, and it was actually fun to work with her.

That evening, after Maddie came home from work, she quickly grabbed her notebook and began writing down everything Eva had told her. It wasn't until she got to the part where Eva was arrested that an essential part of the story hit her—Eva was locked up and probably didn't get a chance to début as a principal dancer in her two ballets. Maddie's heart went out to her. But maybe she did get out in time to dance. Now, she was even more eager to hear the rest of the story.

The next morning, Maddie hurried and mowed two of her neighbors' yards and then went home to change before going to Eva's. Her mother had just returned from practicing dancing as Maddie was about to leave the house.

"How was Eva this morning?" Maddie asked, hoping she hadn't been too worn out from yesterday's talk.

"She was in good spirits," Sandy said. "She thinks it's time I put an ad in the paper and online, announcing dance classes for this fall."

"That's great!" Maddie said. "I'm sure your classes will fill up quickly."

"I hope so," Sandy said. "And I hope I'm ready."

Maddie studied her mother for a moment. She hadn't seen her mother this excited about something in years. "I'm sure you're more than ready, Mom," she said.

A car honking from the driveway made them both look out toward the back door.

"Who in the world is that?" Sandy said.

Maddie chuckled. "Well, it's not Caden, that's for sure. Livie told me he already has a new girlfriend who's been hanging out with him at home now that he's out of the hospital."

Sandy grimaced. "How do you feel about that?"

"I'm okay," Maddie said. "I'm the one who broke up with him. He can see anyone he wants."

"That's very mature of you, dear," Sandy said.

The car honked again, so both Sandy and Maddie walked out the kitchen door and into the driveway. There, standing beside Maddie's beloved red Toyota Corolla, was Matt with a grin on his face.

"My car!" Maddie said, running over to it. She assessed the area that had been damaged. "It looks just like new!"

"I figured you were ready to have your car back," Matt said. "You've been working hard all summer, so you deserve it."

Maddie threw her arms around her dad. "Thanks, Dad! But I haven't paid you for it yet."

Matt looked over at Sandy conspiratorially, and they both smiled. "Our car insurance paid for most of it," he said. "And we covered the deductible. We just wanted you to learn a lesson in taking care of things. And you worked all summer and saved money, so we're proud of you."

"I can give you the money I've saved," Maddie said, backing up to head into the house and get it.

"You don't have to, honey," Matt said. "We want you to keep it and put it in the bank. Hopefully, you'll keep saving your money and will have some extra money when you go off to college."

"Really?" Maddie was stunned. "Are you sure?"

"We're sure, dear," Sandy said. "Believe me, you'll need extra money if you go away to college. It's expensive living on your own."

"Thank you!" Maddie said, hugging first her dad and then her mom. "And I will keep saving. I have a whole year to save more money. Thanks for paying to have my car fixed."

"You're welcome, honey," Matt said.

"Can I drive it now?" Maddie said. "I was just going over to Eva's house."

"Absolutely," Matt said. "But please, don't let Eva or Ginny drive your car." He grinned.

"No one but me will drive this car from now on," Maddie said. She hopped into her car with a big smile on her face. She couldn't wait to show Ginny and Eva her car, the reason she'd worked so hard all summer. And also tell them how great her parents were.

CHAPTER TWENTY-THREE

Eva

Eva pleaded guilty to transporting stolen materials across state borders and serving as Colin's go-between with the dealers. She had no choice. If she went to court and fought it, she risked getting a longer sentence. This way, by cooperating with the authorities, she was given only two years in a medium security prison.

With a lawyer Ray had obtained for her present, she told the detectives what little she knew. She gave them a list of all the parties she and Colin attended so the authorities could match them against the names of people who'd been robbed. She also handed over the diamond necklace Colin had given her. It had been stolen, too, and she no longer wanted it.

In exchange for what she could tell them, the detectives kept their end of the bargain. They kept her name quiet and out of the papers, and there was never any reference to her stage name in any of the files. If someone researched the case years from now, they would never know that Eve Arthur was also

Evalina Ashford, a ballerina for the New York City Ballet.

Eva's mother had flown directly to NYC to see her, what little she was allowed, and stayed in Eva's apartment until the case was resolved. She stood beside her daughter because she knew Eva would never have knowingly participated in such a crime. Bea and Ginny believed that too and visited her at the jail whenever they were allowed.

Thankfully, Colin was caught as he tried to leave town on a train and was prosecuted to the full extent of the law. He went to trial, but there was never any mention of Eva during it. After all Colin had done, he made sure to keep Eva's name out of the papers as well. Eva believed in his own way, he had loved her, just not enough to tell her the truth.

As promised, Gwen called Mr. B that very day that Eva asked her to and explained what was happening. She told Eva later that he'd sounded distraught to hear what Colin had done to ruin Eva's life. But he also promised Gwen he would not tell anyone where Eva had gone. He cared deeply for her and didn't want to tarnish her memory as a ballerina with the company. Everyone at the company who asked was told Eva had walked away from dancing. It happened, so they weren't completely surprised. But the fact that she walked away just as she had become a principal dancer seemed odd to everyone. Yet, eventually, everyone moved on with their own lives and careers and no longer asked about the talented ballerina, Eva.

Eva was sent to a medium security women's prison about an hour north of NYC. She was not considered a danger or an escape risk. She would quietly serve out her time and leave.

Eva made the best of it that she could. She read the books her mother and Ginny sent her and did the job assigned to her each day. In her free time after breakfast each morning, she created her own ballet class in her cell to keep her body in shape. It was nothing like being in Mr. B's class, and she knew her skills were wasting away, but she tried. She needed to hold onto something from her past life, if only to remember who she used to be and who she almost was. She'd studied ballet much too long to have it taken away from her forever.

After Eva had gone to prison, her mother returned to Minnesota, but she wrote to her often. Gwen sent money for Eva's personal needs, which she was thankful for. Eva had lost everything when she lost her job. She'd had very little money because ballerinas didn't dance to become rich—they danced because they loved it. So, most dancers often earned very little to live on.

The first three months at the prison were the hardest for Eva. She had a quiet personality naturally, and being in a place where she knew no one was difficult. No privacy was hard, too. And she missed some of the other dancers and dancing, too. Her whole life had been ballet, and now, it felt strange not to dance for hours a day.

Ginny cried the first time she visited Eva at the prison. They were allowed to sit together in a visiting room, along with other families visiting inmates. Ginny was generally a strong woman, but seeing small, petite Eva in that environment nearly broke her. However, she forced herself to toughen up, and all visits after that, she kept a smile on her face and plenty of family gossip on her lips to entertain Eva.

One Saturday, four months into her sentence, when Eva wasn't expecting a visitor, she was told to go to the visiting room. Eva went and was surprised to see an older man wearing a hat and a suit jacket over a striped western shirt.

"Mr. B! I can't believe you're here!" Eva said excitedly, then dropped her voice. "But you shouldn't be here. Someone might recognize you."

"Ah, dear. So, what if they do?" Balanchine said, grinning at her. "I had to come see if you are okay." He looked around the room, his nose wrinkled in distaste. "How I hate to see you in a place like this."

Tears filled Eva's eyes, and she swiped at them before they could fall. "Thank you for coming. After everything that's happened, I started to think my life with the ballet was only a dream."

Mr. B leaned in closer. "Eva, dear. It was not a dream. You were and are a lovely dancer with so much life left ahead of you. I have not forgotten you, dear. And I never will."

"I'm so sorry I left you in such a bind," Eva said. "But please believe me—I had no idea what Colin was doing. He fooled me just as he fooled all those rich women."

Mr. B sniffed. "Mr. Sleek was not a good person. I know you are innocent, my dear. The little girl I knew who sewed ribbons on pointe shoes for lunch money would not have grown up to be a thief." He shook his head. "No. You were taken in by a con man, through no fault of your own."

His words made Eva feel better. She never wanted to disappoint Mr. B, who'd done so much to give her a dance career. "I guess I should have listened to you from the beginning," Eva said. "Colin was Mr. Sleek after all."

Mr. B gave her one of his knowing grins. "Yes. Everyone should always listen to me. I am always right."

Eva laughed softly.

"I hear you are in here for only two years," Mr. B said, turning serious. "Less now, I suppose. I came to tell you to keep in shape. Practice every day if you can. Because I hope to see you back in the ballet when you are free."

Eva gasped. "Really? Are you sure? Won't people wonder where I was and why I left? Won't they talk?"

Mr. B waved his hand through the air to brush away her worries. "I do not care what others think, and neither should you. Come home when you are done here. You will always be welcome in my dance company."

Eva was so grateful, she wished she could hug Mr. B. His words had given her hope. If she could keep working her body to stay in shape, she'd have a place in his ballet when she left here. Even if it wasn't practical, it was that hope that would help her get through the rest of her days.

* * *

The day Eva was released from prison, her mother and Ray were there to greet her. Even though it had been only two years, Gwen looked much older than before, and Ray had aged as well. Eva felt terrible that she may have been the one to put the dark circles and worry lines under their eyes.

They stayed at Bea's apartment, and Ginny and Marty came over for dinner that night. Ginny hugged Eva for the longest time when she walked inside the apartment.

"I have to make sure this is real," she said in Eva's ear.

Her words warmed Eva's heart. She could hardly believe she was there, too.

Eva was still on twelve months' parole, so her lawyer had obtained special permission for her to move to Minnesota with her mother and Ray. She would live with them for that time and decide what she would do next. Eva was only twenty-three years old, but she felt like she'd lived several lifetimes. She was relieved to be going somewhere where no one knew who she was, so she wouldn't feel shame every day of her life for what had happened to her.

For months after Mr. B's visit to the prison, Eva had worked to keep in dancing form with the hope of returning to the ballet. But as time went on, she realized that going back wasn't a good idea. Everyone would have questions. New dancers would resent an older dancer coming back and taking a spot they wanted. Spite might compel someone to dig deeper and learn the reason why she'd disappeared. Eva couldn't live with that. She didn't want to tarnish the NYCB's reputation or the good reputation of George Balanchine. By the time she was let out of prison, she'd decided not to return to the ballet company. It was a difficult decision, but she knew it was the right one. Dance had been her life since she was five years old. Now, it was gone.

Ray, Gwen, and Eva flew to Minnesota and then drove the four hours north to Cedar Creek, the small town where they lived. When they drove down the long, tree-covered driveway to the lake house, Eva's eyes grew wide. Her mother always called their house a cabin. But what lay before Eva was no cabin—it was a beautiful home with what looked like a tower with windows on one end.

"You're going to love it here," Ray said, smiling over his shoulder at Eva. "And we have a surprise for you."

"Shh! You'll ruin it," Gwen said to her husband, laughing.

The threesome walked up the front steps and through the orange-painted door.

"This place was very 'north country' with its brown exterior and hunter green trim," Gwen said. "I needed a splash of color on the door."

Eva smiled. "I love it."

They walked through a small living room and into the smaller dining room off the kitchen. Wood pocket doors with stained-glass inserts blocked the entrance to the tower room beyond. The glass on the doors depicted Lakeland scenes featuring blue herons, loons, and swans.

"These are beautiful!" Eva said, lightly touching the glass. "So elegant."

"We just love them," Gwen said. "But you'll love what's beyond them." Gwen and Ray went to the middle of the doors and slowly opened them to the side.

Eva gazed past the parting doors into the large room. The ceiling had to be at least twenty feet high, and the windows facing the lake were enormous. A honey-colored hardwood floor spread out in front of her to a stone fireplace on the other end. There were couches and chairs with a big rug underneath in front of the cozy fireplace. It was truly a grand great room.

"It's amazing," Eva said, stepping inside. "So beautiful!" She looked up and saw there was a loft up a short flight of stairs overlooking the living room. "I'll bet the view of the lake from the loft is incredible!"

"We've decided the loft will be your own special place," Gwen said, coming up beside her daughter. "To read, to relax, and to dream. I hope it will inspire you."

"Really?" Eva was overwhelmed with emotion. She'd been living in a small cell for nearly two years. To have this wide-open space to herself would be wonderful! She ran up the stairs and looked around. Shelves on the far wall were filled with books, and there was a cozy nook with a cushy sofa right under the tall windows up there. A small television set sat on a table, too. And the view! The tree-studded yard and lake spread out before her.

An eagle flew by, into the treetops. This was definitely a room to relax and reflect in.

"I love it!" Eva said, looking over the railing at her mother. "Thank you."

She smiled. "Your bedroom is down the hallway at the end, so that you will have a little privacy. But that room upstairs is all yours when you want to have time to yourself. And this room," she spun slowly with her arms wide. "Can be our living room in the evening, and your dance studio during the day."

Eva stared at her mother. "Dance studio?"

"Isn't that wonderful?" Ray asked, looking excited. "Your mom insisted we have the best hardwood floors so you could teach dance in this room. We can set up a few portable ballet barres around the room and slide the furniture out of the way. It's perfect for a dance studio."

Eva walked down the stairs until she was standing in front of Gwen and Ray. "Would you really want your peaceful home to be turned into a noisy dance studio all day?"

"Only if you want to teach ballet," Gwen said quickly. "We're not suggesting you do anything you don't want to do. I just thought that eventually, you'll miss ballet, and what better to do than teach what you know to the next generation. But there's no pressure."

"And we'd love for you to use the room," Ray said. "Heck, I'm out on the lake fishing all summer and off doing things I like all day or tinkering in my shop downstairs in the winter. Noise up here wouldn't bother me at all."

"And I could play piano for your classes," Gwen said. "We haven't bought one yet, but we can any time you're ready."

Eva stood silent as she assessed her surroundings once again. A ballet studio. The room was certainly large enough, and the view would be inspiring. She smiled as she remembered the day Mr. B caught her dancing in one of the studios, making up her own steps as she went.

"Ah. You were choreographing your own ballet. Are you trying to take my job?" Mr. B had said, smiling at her. Well, maybe she couldn't choreograph as well as Mr. B, but she could teach young girls the Balanchine method and send new dancers out into the world, spreading his technique. What a privilege that would be.

Eva smiled at her mother. "I love that idea. Maybe once I'm settled in, we can work on a plan to get the studio started. I need some time to acclimate back to the real world."

Gwen smiled broadly. "Dear, take all the time you need. You have your whole life ahead of you to do whatever you wish."

Eva nodded. Yes. She had a long life ahead of her. And she planned on doing what she loved without exception.

Chapter Twenty-Four

Maddie

Maddie sat next to Eva on the sofa with tears in her eyes. "And now you're going to help my mom live her dream," she said to Eva. "You've come full circle."

Eva nodded. "Yes, dear. Isn't life wonderful?"

Maddie agreed it was. So much had changed since that first day she'd knocked on the ladies' door to ask about lawn mowing. She'd made two new friends whom she adored, and her mother found her passion again."

"I couldn't find any pictures or film of you dancing for the NYCB online," Maddie said. "You're not listed anywhere. It's like you're a ballerina lost in time."

Eva nodded. "There wouldn't be any record of what happened to me since I just disappeared that day I was arrested, and my real name was in the court records. No one knew what happened to me. Only Mr. B, and he kept it quiet, as I asked him to."

"But you stayed connected to Mr. Balanchine all those years," Maddie said. "Since you sent new dancers to him."

"Yes. When I left New York, I told him where I was going, and every so often, I received a NYC postcard from him telling me something funny his cat did or what new ballet he'd created. When I told him I was opening a ballet school and that I'd teach his way of dancing, Mr. B was thrilled. '*Keep my technique alive, dear,*' he'd written. '*And send me your most talented dancers when they are ready.*' So, I did. And I wanted to send your mother to Jerome and Peter, the men who took Mr. B's place after he died, but she didn't want to go. I wish she had, but maybe it wasn't meant to be. Maybe, her future was always supposed to be here, keeping Mr. B's ballet technique alive."

"That's so amazing," Maddie said. Her mind spun as she tried to remember every word Eva was saying. "And it was Mr. Balanchine who gave you that beautiful cane."

Eva nodded. "Yes. He was always generous with his things. He grew up with nothing during the revolution, and he didn't care if he had anything, even when he was famous all over the world. He lived simply, and his first love was always ballet."

"I'm so happy you told me your story," Maddie said. "And I'm sorry that you had to go through so much pain and not realize your dream of becoming a principal dancer. That must have been hard to accept. You were so close."

"It was, at first. But I realized that my place was here," Eva said, smiling. "And I've never regretted teaching others to dance. It's been a pleasure."

"How did Ginny come to be here?" Maddie asked.

"I can answer that," Ginny said, poking her head out the kitchen door. "Marty and I were married for thirty-five years, and he passed away. We were never able to have children, and once he was gone, and my parents had passed away by then, too,

Eva invited me to come here to live and be her piano player."
She rolled her eyes. "She knew I hated playing, but I was pretty
good, and I was ready for a change. So, here we are, two old
biddies, living out our lives."

"We're not old biddies," Eva said, sitting up straighter.
"We're elegant, mature ladies."

"Call it what you will," Ginny said, looking over at Maddie.
"But the truth is, Eva saved me from a lonely life, and I've been
grateful to her ever since."

Maddie smiled. "I'm glad you two are together. I couldn't
imagine it any other way."

"My mother and Ray had passed away before Ginny came
here, too," Eva added. "So, I was happy to have the company.
And Ginny's a pretty good cook."

"Pretty good? Why, I'm the best," Ginny said, winking at
Maddie.

Maddie laughed. She turned to Eva. "Do you know what
happened to Colin Hughes? Or, maybe I should call him by his
real name, Anthony Rumsey."

Eva looked pensive. "I know that he went on trial for theft
and was found guilty. I don't know how many years they put
him away for, though. And I never heard from him again."
She looked into Maddie's eyes. "I did love him, and I want to
believe that he loved me, too, at least for a time. But he wasn't
good for me. I think you know exactly what I mean."

Maddie thought about Caden and all he'd put her through.
"Yes. Maybe not to the extent of what you went through,
but I do know what you mean. I'm glad I left my boyfriend
before something terrible happened that would change my life
completely."

"I'm glad you did, too," Eva said softly. "There is so much

waiting for you out there. Make smart choices, and you can accomplish anything you desire."

"Thank you, Eva," Maddie said. "For sharing your story with me. It has meant so much more to me than you can imagine."

"I knew you were the right person to share it with," Eva said. "The day you came here, I saw it in your eyes."

"My goodness!" Ginny said from the kitchen doorway. "It's getting awfully gooey in here. I swear I'm watching one of those sickly-sweet movies from that card company channel."

Maddie and Eva both laughed.

"Okay. We'll stop before you get nauseous," Maddie said, standing up. She walked over to Ginny. "But not until I get a hug from you for all the delicious lunches you've made for me." She reached over and pulled Ginny into a hug. Ginny didn't resist.

"Why, you make it sound like you're leaving us forever," Ginny said, composing herself after she'd pulled away. "Summer isn't over yet. You still have to mow our lawn and weed the garden."

"I will keep doing that until winter," Maddie said. "But school starts in two weeks, so I won't be able to visit as often." She looked from Ginny to Eva. "I'll miss spending time here."

"Ah, pooh!" Ginny said. "Your mom is going to be here some nights teaching dance, and I'm sure you'll tag along. So, don't be so dramatic." She turned and walked back into the kitchen.

"Ah, Ginny," Eva said, standing and walking Maddie to the door. "She can be prickly."

"I wouldn't want her to be any other way," Maddie said. She hugged the tiny lady with the cane, being careful not to break her. Eva seemed so fragile, yet she'd been such a strong person her entire life.

"Don't forget to finish writing my story," Eva said, her eyes twinkling.

"I'm going home right now and writing all night," Maddie assured her. "I'll see you soon."

"I'm counting on it," Eva said.

Maddie stepped out onto the porch and saw her car there waiting for her. She sighed. All this happened because Caden crashed her car. Maybe she should thank him for that after all.

* * *

Maddie went home and did exactly what she told Eva she would do. She wrote for hours, trying to remember every bit of Eva's story as her pen flew across the page. As soon as she was done, she planned to type up the story in manuscript format, edit it, and maybe edit it some more. She knew she wasn't a professional writer yet, but she'd do her best for Eva.

The last two weeks of summer went by quickly. Maddie had lawns to mow, work at the Freeze, and college applications to fill out. Livie had already decided she wanted to attend the University of Denver. She said she felt the most comfortable with the coach there and knew she could do well for their gymnastics team. So, Maddie filled out the DU application first and did her best on her admission essay. She actually used her story from that summer for the essay, telling how she matured that summer and learned a life lesson: taking responsibility for her actions and opening herself to listening to the people around her. She hoped the essay would prove she could write well so she would be accepted into the creative writing program.

The first day of her senior year, Maddie and Livie walked past Caden and his new girlfriend, Amanda. Caden had a walking cast by then, but was getting around pretty well while his girlfriend carried his books. He also looked much better and healthier than the last time Maddie had seen him.

Caden looked up and stared right at her for a moment, then slowly smiled. He nodded, and she did, too. To Maddie, it was a relief. She'd been afraid Caden hated her after breaking up with him, but he'd moved on, and she had, too. Maybe senior year wouldn't be as difficult as she'd thought.

The first night Sandy held dance classes at Eva's house, Maddie was there for support. She'd helped her mother earlier in the week to move the furniture and set the ballet barres along the windows and walls. They had set up a record player, because her mom was old-school, and Sandy had spent hours picking the perfect classical music for each class. She set up a dance routine for children ages five to seven, and another, more difficult routine for dancers over eight years old. To her surprise, a few older women also wanted to take ballet as an exercise class, so Sandy set that up as well. She was teaching two classes a night, two nights a week, and three classes on Saturdays. She'd never expected to have enough students to fill the classes, but the minute word got out that there was a new ballet teacher in town, her phone rang off the hook.

Maddie and Lily were both there that first night, and Lily actually wanted to take a class with the older students, too. Lily thought ballet would give her an edge in gymnastics, and, not surprisingly, she was good at dancing. Maddie watched in wonder at her little sister. Whatever Lily chose to do in life, she would certainly succeed.

"So, what do you think of your mother as a ballet teacher?"

Eva asked quietly as she and Maddie watched through a crack in the pocket doors.

"She's amazing," Maddie said with pride. "She's exactly where she's supposed to be."

Eva looked over at Maddie, and the two exchanged a look. They both knew that they were all exactly where they were supposed to be.

EPILOGUE

One Year Later

Maddie was almost packed and ready to go. She was leaving for college the next day with her car packed to the brim. Her father was going to drive with her to Colorado and help her get settled, then fly home. Her mother was sorry she couldn't go, but school was starting soon, and her dance classes already had, so she couldn't get the time off to go along. Livie was already at DU because the gymnastics coach had required his team members to be there a week early. Maddie couldn't wait to go. She and Livie were lucky enough to room together in the dorms, and they were planning on having a fun freshman year.

But first, Maddie had one last important thing to do before she left.

The scent of fall was in the air as Maddie walked the short distance to the big house carrying a gift for Eva. When she reached the driveway, Maddie stopped and gazed down the long path. She smiled as she remembered that first time she walked down to the house, scared to death that the rumors were true that two old witches lived there. The truth couldn't have been more different. What she found down that driveway was friendship and an inspiring story. What she'd also found was her future.

The orange door opened before Maddie even made it to the top step.

"I told Eva you wouldn't leave without saying goodbye," Ginny said smugly. "She was so worried she wouldn't see you for another nine months."

Maddie smiled. "I couldn't leave without saying goodbye to my two favorite people."

"Oh, pish! You're still laying it on thick. That's why you'll be a good writer." Ginny's words were said with a grin on her face. "Well, come in. Eva's in the dance studio, enjoying the fall view out the windows."

Maddie walked through the living room to the dining room and then through the open pocket doors. The room was set up for dance class tonight, the portable barres strung out against the walls and tall windows. Eva stood at the big windows, cane in hand, gazing out at the lake as it sparkled in the sunshine. She turned, and a smile spread across her face.

"You came," Eva said with glee. She waited patiently as Maddie came up beside her.

"I couldn't leave without saying goodbye," Maddie said. "After all, you had a hand in helping me decide my future."

"Oh, no, dear. You made those decisions all by yourself. I was just here to give you a little encouragement," Eva said.

"I was here to feed you," Ginny said behind them. "That must count for something."

Maddie laughed. "It counts for a lot. I loved my lunches here."

Ginny stood a bit straighter, and her chin rose with pride.

"I brought you something," Maddie said, turning back to Eva. She handed her a thick manila envelope.

"What's this?" Eva asked, looking surprised.

"It's your story," Maddie said. "I wrote as much of it as I could remember, and I've polished it up the best I knew how. I hope I got everything right."

"Ah, dear," Eva said gently. "I'm sure you did a wonderful job. But I don't need to read this—I lived it." She handed the manuscript back to Maddie.

"That's true," Maddie said, taken aback. "But it's your story."

Eva smiled. "No, dear. It's your story now."

Chills ran up Maddie's spine. "I don't understand."

"When I told you my story, I gave it to you. Do whatever you wish with it. Use it as inspiration for a novel or place it in a drawer for all eternity. It belongs to you now."

Maddie accepted the envelope back. She reached down and hugged Eva, tears filling her eyes. "Thank you for all you've done for me," she whispered. "And for my mother. She's the happiest she's ever been."

Eva hugged her back. "It was my pleasure, dear. There comes a time when we all need to give back. Remember that."

Maddie nodded. When she turned to hug Ginny goodbye, she saw the older woman wiping her eyes with a handkerchief.

"I'm not crying," Ginny insisted. "It's...it's dusty in here."

Maddie walked over and hugged her. "Thank you for everything."

"We were happy to help," Ginny said softly. When she pulled away, she was all business again. "But you'll be back to mow our lawn next summer, won't you? You were the best person we've ever had."

Maddie laughed. "I'm sure I'll be back, and I will definitely mow your lawn."

Eva walked her to the door, and they hugged once more. "Go out there and make me proud," Eva said.

"I'll do my best," Maddie said. She waved to the women as she descended the stairs. As she walked slowly up the driveway, Maddie glanced at Eva's story in her hand. Maybe, someday, she'd share Eva's story. Or maybe not. Whatever happened in the years to come, Maddie knew she'd never forget Evalina Ashford, George Balanchine's ballerina.

-The End-

ABOUT THE AUTHOR

Deanna Lynn Sletten is the author of THE LAST LADY OF THE SILVER SCREEN, MRS. WINCHESTER'S BIOGRAPHER, THE ONES WE LEAVE BEHIND, THE WOMEN OF GREAT HERON LAKE, FINDING LIBBIE, MAGGIE'S TURN, and several other titles. She writes heart-warming women's fiction, captivating historical fiction, a murder mystery series, and romance novels with unforgettable characters. She has also written one middle-grade novel that takes you on the adventure of a lifetime.

Deanna is married and has two grown children. When not writing, she enjoys peaceful walks in the woods around her property with her beautiful Australian Shepherd, traveling, photography, and relaxing on the lake.

Connect with Deanna at her website: deannalsletten.com

www.ingramcontent.com/pod-product-compliance
Lightning Source LLC
Chambersburg PA
CBHW071303250626
47159CB00004B/1295